SOUND OF REDEMPTION
BAND IN THE WIND, BOOK 2

Cover Design and Interior Format
© **KILLION**
THE
GROUP, INC.

SOUND *of* REDEMPTION

BAND IN THE WIND
BOOK 2

William John Rostron

For my parents
William John Rostron Sr. (Bill)
And
Josephine Paradiso Rostron (Peppy)

"I may be wrong, but I won't be wrong always."

~ Ten Years After

PROLOGUE

"Strangers When We Meet" - Reprise
- The Smithereens

June 8, 1990

MARIA ROMANO WAS GOING HOME. She was not travelling to her comfortable suburban house in Floral Park, but rather to the home of her soul, the place where she grew up – Cambria Heights. Her family had been one of the first to move from there in the great "white flight" of the 1960s. Her racist parents had insisted that once the neighborhood became integrated it would become "hell on Earth" for white people.

However, what Maria saw before her were rows of old, but nicely kept houses. The neighborhood had survived, indeed thrived. *If this was hell, then make me a sinner.* Still she felt trepidation. Was it the latent fear of others that her father had worked very hard to instill in her or something else? Though she now lived less than ten miles away, this was her first trip back in decades. She realized that it was the memories of her time in the Heights that she could not face. This was the place of her childhood and the happiest moments of her life. This is where she had met and shared her secrets with her best friend Diane. This was where she played in the streets with a cadre of fun-loving neighbors. And this was where she had fallen in love with Johnny Cipp.

As tears swelled up in her eyes, reality intruded on her memories. Diane was dead, as were all of Johnny's friends and bandmates. They had all been caught up in the madness of Mad Guy Provenzano's murder spree during what Johnny had called "a season in hell." Yes, Johnny himself had written that in the journal that she held in her hand. It had come to her house that very morning and she had read it through tear-stained eyes. After more than twenty years, Maria finally had answers. She now knew that Johnny had not died in 1967. This incredible revelation, after all her years of waiting and wondering, could have been an emotionally crippling event. But she had no time for self-serving feelings. The note that came in the same package as the book had instructions. She had a job to do.

As Maria knocked on Riet's door, she knew that life would never be the same for either of them. Riet had no reason to know Maria and she had no reason to believe what she was about to be told. But Maria had to make her believe. Riet had to understand that it was a matter of life or death.

PART
1

"Wake Me, Shake Me"
– The Blues Project

1

The Other Side of Life:
"Stairway to Heaven"
– Led Zeppelin

Four Months Before
February 14, 1990

I RISE FROM THE SAND AND take a few steps into the chilly waters of the Zachary Taylor Beach. I can almost see their faces in the moonlit clouds. I can hear their voices in the wind. They are waiting for me. I hear them calling my name. *"Johnny! Johnny!"*

The coolness of the saltwater tickles my toes.

I can hear Gio and Jimmy Mac singing in harmony. My drummer is still wearing that eternal grin that so enthralled the ladies. Gio gives me thumbs up and starts laughing.

The water now surrounds my calves and splashes on my knees.

I won't throw the book out into the waves. Instead, I will

send it back to the waiting sand. Perhaps someone will find it?

My thighs feel the tingle of the salt water as I start to approach the crashing waves.

And Tinman is wailing on the organ. He looks up and takes time to wink at me. He is playing our music and loving it. He puts his head down to concentrate on a solo part. Next to him is Bracko and he too is smiling. No! He is laughing with wild abandon as I have never seen him before. There are no bruises on him. He nods at me and returns to bending the strings of his Strat. I can hear their distant voices calling me, *"Johnny! Johnny!"*

The water now straddles my waist and starts to caress my shoulders.

They beckon me. The band needs a bass player to give them a backbeat . . . and a friend to share their joy. I will join them, and again we will be complete. We will make music . . . and we will laugh . . . and the band will again be together . . . in the wind . . . forever.

2

The Other Side of Life:
"And the Tide Rushes In"
- *The Moody Blues*

"NO, JOHNNY, NO," YELLED PADRE into the violent surf as he read the final entry. He scanned the crashing waves in hopes of seeing his friend. Despite the fact that the cover was titled "Journal of Johnny Cipp," Padre knew it had been written by the person he knew as Jack Paradise.

He had found Jack lying on this very beach last spring. *Key-wasted* was a term that the locals used to describe those that had hit rock bottom in the downward spiral of drug and alcohol abuse that was so common in America's southernmost outpost. Padre had worked with Jack and helped him on his way to sobriety. He had encouraged him to start work on this journal.

Johnny had fled his Cambria Heights' home in Queens, New York to save his life. The other four members of his band, Those Born Free, had been murdered by the local crime lord, Mad Guy Provenzano. Yet, "Jack" had not just fled his home, he had run away from all those he loved and who loved him in return.

Padre knew that Jack blamed himself for the deadly rampage of Mad Guy. A strange confluence of events had led the then seventeen-year-old to represent the entire band as old enough to perform at a local club. When this fact led to a police raid on that club, all of his bandmates had been arrested. Provenzano, as the club's owner, had been disgraced in front of the capos of his mob. His retribution had taken the lives of the rest of the band one at a time.

Johnny had also left behind the love of his life, Maria Romano. When his efforts to convince himself that his flight had been for her own good failed to assuage his guilty conscience, he spiraled into a decades-long descent into hell. Though humble by nature, Padre understood that it was only his intervention and Johnny's hard work that had led to the salvation of his friend. But had it? Once sober, "Jack" had tried to fulfill Step 9 of his AA program - *make amends to those you have harmed.*

While attempting that task, Johnny had come to discover that both of his parents had passed away, brokenhearted that they never knew what had happened to their son. To compound his misery, Johnny had also recently found out that while he was wallowing in his despair, Maria had moved on without him. She was now happily married and had two children and a successful career.

If these heartbreaks were not enough, there was the question of Riet. His best friend, Gio, had saved Johnny from certain death at the hands of Mad Guy Provenzano. And how had Johnny repaid him? As Gio took his last breaths, he made just one request of his best friend—go to Riet and tell her that he (Gio) had loved her to the very last moments of his life. Johnny had never spoken to Riet. Johnny had never told Maria he was leaving. Johnny had never said goodbye to his parents. All this weighed on him, and Padre still remembered his final conversation with Johnny. He had come to the priest earlier that day.

"You OK, Jack?"

"No, Padre. I haven't been OK for a very long time."

"But, Jack, you worked so hard with your recovery."

"Padre, I know that hiding from the world and myself for all these years was not a good thing, but . . . "

"But what, Johnny?"

"With sobriety comes reality. With reality comes understanding. With understanding comes responsibility. And with responsibility comes guilt. Padre, nothing is masking my guilt now. I'm feeling every shitty bit of it. Bracko, Tinman, Jimmy Mac . . . and Gio. Oh, God, how I let Gio down. . . and Maria . . . and my parents . . . and Riet."

"C'mon. Jack, you've come so far," responded Padre.

"Have I, Padre?"

For one of the few times in his life, Padre just could not come up with the right words to bring Jack back from the brink.

"Padre, I have to go play at Reilly's now."

"Good, good. Music has always been your 'doctor,' and you'll feel better after a few tunes."

"Ah, yes, my Music Doctor," he spoke softly. Padre understood what he meant. His imaginary creation, the Music Doctor, always inspired Johnny to sing relevant songs to the situations that he found himself living. As he left the church, Johnny knew he could not tell the Padre what the Music Doctor had been whispering in his ear all that afternoon. There would be one song in his set tonight that had not been there in a while. If Padre had listened closely, he would have heard the feint strains of Johnny humming "Fear the Reaper."

As Padre peered out across the moonlit waters, he knew he had failed. He had not really saved "Jack." The return to sobriety had been too much, perhaps too soon, for the real person who had written this damp journal he held in his hands. Was Padre too late to stop Johnny's date with the Grim Reaper?

If Jack had decided to end his life, it could not have been too long ago—and it could not have been too far away. The proof lay in his hands. Johnny must have written his final epitaph in the journal while still near enough the shore to fling the composition book to the waiting sand.

All these thoughts went through Padre's brain as he scanned the waters off Zachary Taylor Beach. He realized exactly who he was searching for when his voice unconsciously screamed for "Johnny" rather than "Jack."

"Johnny. Johnny!"

3

The Other Side of Life:
"Knockin' On Heaven's Door"
- Bob Dylan

"JOHNNY, JOHNNY," SCREAMED PADRE OUT into the crashing surf. His eyes peered out from the shore for any sign of his friend. He knew that somewhere out in the darkness was the man who had written his final words in the book that he held. It was then that he spotted a fleeting glimpse of a half-submerged Johnny and ran into the crashing surf.

They beckon me. The band needs a bass player to give them a backbeat . . . and a friend to share their joy. I will join them, and again we will be complete. We will make music . . . and we will laugh . . . and the band will again be together . . . in the wind . . . . forever.

"Hold on, Johnny, I'm coming," yelled Padre as he challenged the increasingly violent waves. Johnny either could not hear him or was ignoring him. Still, he slowly plowed through the resistant surf toward his now floundering friend. Johnny could not answer as a powerful wave knocked him underwater and propelled his body to the sandy bottom.

Johnny heard no more instruments playing. He saw no more band playing in the wind. Yet, he did hear a voice calling to him as he slipped into unconsciousness.

———◆———

"*Hey asshole, what do you think you are doing?*"
Johnny opened his eyes to see Gio in front of him.
"*I said, what do you think you're doing?*"
"*You can't be here, Gio. You're . . .*"
"*Dead? Good fuckin' guess, numbnuts.*"
"*Gio, that means that I'm . . .*"
"*Yeah, . . . well, almost, Johnny, almost. How does it feel being the mayor of Crazytown?*"
Johnny took a closer look and saw the rope burn etched on Gio's throat, each moment of torture of his schoolyard lynching ingrained in his skin. He pushed out his hand to touch it and Gio pulled away.
"*You got that saving me,*" *whispered Johnny.*
"*Well, yeah. Now don't you feel like a fuckin' prick, Johnny?*"
"*I have for almost twenty-three years.*"
"*No, no, no! Shit-for-brains, you don't get it. They were going to kill me anyway. That isn't what pisses me off. It's what you did afterward.*"
"*What did I do?*"
"*Nothing, Johnny, god-dammit, nothing. You didn't live happily ever after with Maria. You didn't tell my parents I died. And you never told Riet that I loved her to the end. You did fucking nothing with the time we bought for you. And now . . .*"
"*Now what, Gio?*"
"*You know, Johnny, in your journal you hinted that a few of us weren't the sharpest tacks. Now, look at you.*"
"*What do you mean? What do you know about my journal?*"

"Johnny, Johnny, Johnny," said Gio looking at his wrist at a make-believe watch. "By my calculations, you only have a few seconds more. And Johnny, news alert! I'm dead; I can't really be talking to you. So why the hell should it amaze you that I know what's in your journal? Shithead! Do you understand what exactly is happening here?"

"Gio, I miss you. I miss all the guys. I miss Maria. I'll . . . I'll be with you guys soon."

"No, Johnny, you won't. We don't want you. Not this way."

"But after what I did . . . I let you all down."

"Yeah, blah, blah, blah. I know you're so guilty. Blah, blah, blah. How many fuckin' times did you write that in your journal?"

"But I am, Gio."

"Blah, blah, blah," said Gio putting his hands over his ears until Johnny stopped talking. He then pointed to the imaginary watch again and added, "Tick, tick, tick."

"Gio, it's too late. It's too late for Maria and me . . . it's too late for everything."

"OK, so Maria moved on. I might add she did that after waiting ten years for you. But doesn't she deserve to at least know that you are alive? Don't you owe her that?" Gio then looked down at Johnny's pinkie. Johnny followed his gaze down to the silver ring on his finger.

"Send it to her, Johnny, send it to her."

"And what the hell will that do?"

"Answer her questions. Give her some closure — an ending to your story."

"But even if I did that, I can never make it right with you guys,"

"Johnny, what were the last words I said to you? You know, the last words that you ever heard my living, breathing, real self say to your face?"

"I . . . I can't say them, Gio."

"OK, I will. I said, 'Do something good with your life.'"

"It's too late now, Gio," Johnny said, now pointing to Gio's

imaginary watch.
"*No, Johnny, it's not!*" *said Gio, pointing upward.*

———◆———

Padre's arm reached through dark murky water and found Johnny's hand. He pulled with all his strength and soon the unconscious body broke through to the air. Johnny was breathing, barely. Padre needed to get his dying friend to solid ground where he could give him proper CPR.

"*Do something good with your life, Johnny, something good,*" *said the fading voice of Gio as oxygen started to circulate through his arteries.*

"*I will,*" *answered Johnny though his real voice uttered no words.*
"*And Johnny . . . *"
"*Yeah, Gio?*"
"*You better take care of my goddamn guitar.*"
"*OK, Gio,*" *whispered Johnny.*

"What did you say?" said a confused Padre, but Johnny still remained oblivious to the real world.

———◆———

On the shore, Johnny opened his eyes and looked up.
"I've got to get you to a hospital," said Padre upon seeing Johnny's blank stare.
"No, no. I'm good."
"The hell you are," said Padre.
"Hey, watch the language. Are you allowed to say 'hell?' You know blasphemy and all that?" Johnny actually smiled.
"Are you sure you went to twelve years of Catholic school? Blasphemy is irreverence toward God. Last time I looked, hell wasn't in his zip code."
"But I was almost there . . . wasn't I?"

"Where?"

"You know . . . hell?"

"Johnny, that's between you and Him. You want some orange juice?"

"Damn orange juice again. You're so predictable, Padre."

"What? You want me to carry around a virgin pina colada?"

"Now you're talking, Padre." Johnny struggled to rise to his own two feet and Padre joined him.

"You OK, Johnny?"

"Yeah, I'm breathing good and everything seems to be working."

"Johnny, that's not what I mean. You know . . . up there?" and Padre pointed to Johnny's head.

"Like I told you this afternoon, Padre, I haven't been OK up there in a very long time. But I'm going to try and change that."

"What are you going to do now, Johnny?"

"I don't know exactly," said Johnny with a questioning expression on his face. He looked out over the water. The wind had started to dissipate the clouds that had once held his vision of his lost band. He squinted to see better and thought that he might just have caught a glimpse of Gio as his smiling image faded into nothingness. "But it's going to be something good . . ." He winked at the moonlit sky and repeated, "something damn good."

4

Journal of Johnny Cipp

Entry #92

"You May Be Right, I May Be Crazy"
- *Billy Joel*

DO I TRULY UNDERSTAND WHAT I almost did? No. I still don't know what I was thinking on the beach yesterday. Hell, I don't know what I'm thinking at this very moment.

I promised Padre to give this damn book (now slightly water-damaged) another chance. What do you write about after you almost did away with yourself? Padre said to write about what I'm feeling. Shame? Remorse? Either of those would be better than disappointment which unfortunately is slipping into my mental state.

I didn't tell Padre about Gio's appearance while I fought oxygen deprivation. I didn't want him to think that I was crazy. Or is that crazier than he already thinks I am? Gio made some good points. (Like I said, I'm crazy). It just took me twenty-three years to catch on to what he said to me as he walked to his death.

"Do something good. Make us all proud."

Did it take me almost dying to understand—to truly listen to Gio, or to believe him? My whole journal up until this point has been about understanding what I had done wrong. Only now do I realize that I must do something about it. I must find redemption. I can't do anything for the band. I can't do it for Maria or my parents or Riet. Yet, I will have to do something to prove that my survival was not in vain. Did I have to almost kill myself to figure this out? I mean what good have I done in this world? I'm going to look for the positives in my life. What are my accomplishments?

Still thinking . . .

Oh, yeah, I'm not drunk or dead. Does that count?

Entry #93

"The Walk of Life"
- Dire Straits

Padre thinks I am on to something. Hell, Padre feels anything I do that doesn't have to do with drinking, drugs, or death is good. Yet, he is skeptical that walking is the answer.

"Really, Padre, I will do more and more walking each day and the health of my body and mind will improve."

"Johnny . . . Jack, . . . as long as you are not walking to any beach location, I'm good with it."

"Padre, you know better. The beach wasn't the problem. The problem was me."

"I guess you're right. You could off yourself just about anywhere."

"Gee, thanks for the vote of confidence."

"Just sayin'." Padre let a small smile form. "Just sayin'."

"Really, I think this is the answer."

"How about some orange juice for some energy?"

"Padre, you've got to get over this obsession with OJ."

"Just supporting the Florida economy, you know."

I drank his damn orange juice and started my walk down Truman Avenue, dead center of town—not near any beaches!

That lasted a day. It is the third week of February, peak snowbird season. Up North, they call it Presidents Week. I guess down here we don't love our presidents as much as up there because we only have Presidents Day. That doesn't stop the influx of vacationers from flooding our streets. I need somewhere else to walk, some place where there are no distractions to my mind or physical obstacles to my body.

All I need is to get out in the country and breathe some fresh air. I guess if Key West is my city, then any location east of mile marker 5 is the country. Therefore, tomorrow, filled with enthusiasm and high expectations, I will set off to some higher numbers.

Entry #94

"Honesty"
- *Billy Joel*

I went to an AA meeting last night. I dreaded it. It wasn't that I didn't think I really needed it. I just didn't want to face my sponsor, Cal. I think trying to end my life genuinely qualifies as not following the program. More than that, I let him down.

I didn't meet Cal at my first meeting last August. It was only after about three trips to the church basement I finally got up the nerve to speak. Of course, when you are hiding out and living under an assumed name, it is impossible to be perfectly honest about why you turned to substance abuse. Yet, I did the best I could to recount some of my early trials and tribulations.

After that meeting, he approached me about being my sponsor. I don't exactly know what made him think there was a connection. Here I was this medium-sized, skinny white guy with some remnants of my New York City accent and upbringing still finding the light of day. And then there's Cal, a tall, athletically built black man whose speech gave proof that he was from somewhere in the Deep South. Someday he will tell me why he picked me.

That was last August. I have bared my soul to him. While I never told the facts of my Johnny Cipp existence, I let him in on all my feelings, except the suicidal ones that came out a few days ago. And so, last night could have been ugly. It wasn't. I should have known that he was above that. The conversation was interesting.

———◆———

"Did I let you down, Cal?"

"Jack, you almost ended your life, and you're worried that you might've hurt my feelings? Are you nuts?"

"By definition, yeah. I tried to kill myself. I might add that I did it while listening to an imaginary band playing in the clouds. I think I qualify."

"I'm sorry. I didn't mean . . . "

"Don't sweat it, Cal. It's just your guilt talking. You know that you're officially a failure as a sponsor."

"Jack, I—I—"

"Cal, I'm just messin' with ya. This was all me. You've been great. More than I deserve."

"Thanks, for letting me off the hook. I mean, to be honest, I have screwed up once before while advising someone."

"Yeah, how?"

"No, it's a long story for another day."

"C'mon, I really need to hear about someone else's failures. It'll cheer me up."

"Jack, you're a sick puppy."

"I know, Cal. I know. Humor me."

"OK. About twenty years ago, my brother Hank asked me to be Godfather to his son Lawrence."

"How could you screw that up? It's just a ceremonial thing, mostly just religious shit."

"In theory, I am responsible for making sure about the kid's religious well-being."

"In theory?"

"You know, that he grows up on the straight and narrow. Follows the Bible and all that good stuff."

"If you say so."

"Well, then the wiseass kid goes and gets married by a witch and even goes as far as having demonic decorations as centerpieces on the tables."

"You're kidding me, Cal, right?"

"Jack, I shit you not. I'm guessing that someday I'll have to answer to a higher authority."

"Ha, I'm only your second worst screw up. Strike two on you, Cal. One more and you are out of the 'advising' business."

"Strike two, yeah, interesting analogy. Anyway, my point is that I'm not an expert on this whole sponsor thing. I'm playing it by ear and just trying to be there for you."

"And I shut you out at my most desperate time of need. I'll work on that.

"So now what?"

"Well, I was thinking of doing a great deal of walking to physically help myself and give me time to think."

"Haven't you been doing that while you were writing in

the journal? You know – thinking?"

"Well, I was writing about what happened to me . . . and my friends and trying to figure out what I did wrong to screw up their lives."

"And?"

"And what, Cal?"

"Did you figure out how you screwed up their lives?"

"Well, some of them are dead, but you know I've told you that I can't go into details on any of that."

"That's OK. I don't need to know the details. But do you ever think about those that are still around and what happened to them?"

"There is no way of me knowing. They are far away . . . and it was a long, long time ago."

"I didn't ask, 'Do you know what happened to them?' I asked, 'Do you ever think about what happened to them?'"

"Hmm, I guess you're right. It's something to think about during those long walks."

"Long walks? What are you up to—like a whole quarter of a mile?"

"Well, yeah. But I have ambitions on breaking the four-minute quarter-mile."

"You work on that."

"Cal?"

"Yeah?"

"Demonic centerpieces . . . really?"

"Little devils in tuxes and black wedding dresses. I kid you not."

"Black wedding dresses?"

"Yeah, but the horns went really nice with the veils."

PART
2

"Time Passages"
- Al Stewart

5

Journal of Johnny Cipp:

Entry #95

"Time Passages"
- *Al Stewart*

I WENT TO MILE MARKER 20. It's familiar turf. I pulled off to the side of the road onto a coral and dirt patch that acted as a pseudo-parking lot for would-be anglers of Bow Channel. As I exited my car, I walked out onto the bridge that connected Sugarloaf Key and Cudjoe Key. I have been in this area many times because this is also the location of Mangrove Mama's, a hot spot for Keys' musical acts. I'd spent many nights playing that venue. Somehow, this seemed like just the right place to start my new life. After wrecking my body at Mangrove Mama's, I figured the place owed me something. Why, I don't know.

After procrastinating at the bridge for a few minutes, I started to jog. OK, let's be honest. I was going at a pace just faster than standing still. My exercise program consisted of walking across the Bow Channel fishing bridge at a pace that allowed me time to think but required very little cardiovascular stimulation. This quarter-mile exertion was doing a good job of clearing my head as I gazed at the azure blue water of the inlet and the mangrove trees that were encroaching on its shores.

As my mind cleared and the stillness of the water allowed me to think, I decided that as I trained my body for whatever lay ahead I would also challenge my mind. Cal had made sense. I knew that I could never make anything up to the people I hurt, yet they deserved my thoughts. Each day I would focus on one or more of the people I had left behind—the good and the bad. Perhaps, this would give me clarity. With that clarity, redemption might be found.

The Music Doctor did not fail me. If I'm going to reminisce about the fate of everyone I knew so long ago is there a better title than "Time Passages"? What happened to them in the last twenty-three years? Yes, all of them. I know that Maria has married and has children, but has it been easy for her? I wondered if she had just moved on without further thought to the love we had shared.

Or has she suffered?

As I walked along the mangroves, I thought of our love. I thought of all the fantasies that had crossed my mind in the last two decades. So many songs overtook my emotions. I started to hum "Wonderful Tonight" and relive my ever-recurring dream that Gio and I and our wives are middle aged and having good times together. I do that quite often even when I am not walking.

As I arrived at the part of Clapton's song where he sang, "how much I love you," I realized that I still did love her—and miss her. I know it's all a fantasy. But I came to the realization that despite my love, I can never have her again. That is my fault. From my walk today, I gave myself that closure, that understanding that I had lost it all forever. But what about her? I have no way of knowing what Maria's life has been like. What had the passage of time done to her?

6

Time Passages:
"Lost Little Girl"
– *The Doors*

1967 – 1990

SHE PULLED UP TO THE house after a very long day of teaching English at New Hyde Park High School. Her charges just didn't seem to grasp the concept of where to use an apostrophe in the possessive form of nouns. She had been fighting the good fight to make her students into better writers since she had graduated college. As tough as it was, she loved teaching, and she loved what her whole life had become. Between her salary and that of her husband Jason's New York City police pay, they were living better than she had ever thought would be possible while growing up on the streets of Queens. With her children now attending school in quaint Floral Park, her future was set.

It had not always been this way. After graduating high school, she had lost focus and drifted into years of uncertainty and doubt. Torn away from all of her neighborhood friends to live in a nicer area, Maria never felt like she belonged anywhere. Though she continued to travel to the same high school, that journey was now much longer, not to mention lonelier. The one bright spot in her life had been her boyfriend, Johnny. Somehow, they had stayed close in their hearts even though the physical distance between them had grown. Maria had known this was a sure sign that their love would be forever. The fact that they would be attending college together had been the decisive factor. Together they would beat the odds.

Then Johnny was gone. Not a note. Not a word. Nothing. Her world crashed down around her, and there was no one to console her in her time of despair. With the death of Diane, she had no more real friends, and for this, she blamed her parents. Their move "for her sake" had only driven a wedge between them that had never healed. Talking to them was not an option. If they didn't care that the family's move had taken her away from the love of her life, why would they care if that boy had now gone missing? Not only missing but if some of the rumors from the old neighborhood were true, he was now presumed dead.

She hung around for a while after high school graduation, all the time balancing her worry about Johnny with her hatred for her parents. By the following January, she had dropped out of college and was gone. Pushed by her parents to do something with her life, she did. She ran away. With no particular goal, she meandered through a series of trivial jobs and locations. In accord with the mantra of the times, she dropped out of life. Many club nights that involved entirely too much drinking gave way to other pharmaceuticals. Maria had not been able to commit to anyone or anything since that summer of 1967 when she had lost Johnny. No man could ever replace him.

Maria's experiences had been diverse. She had cleaned toilets at Wrigley Field, Chicago and at night had searched out the blues clubs in hopes that she would find that Johnny had followed the music to its roots. She had been a hippy during the "Summer of Love" in San Francisco until she became disillusioned by the hypocrisy of most of her peers. In Las Vegas, she had been a cocktail waitress until her boss got a bit too friendly and she reacted with a good, swift kick to his balls. Eventually, she found herself penniless and stranded on a desolate section of I-40 in Arizona.

That hot summer afternoon in August of 1971 had been the time when her life had started to turn around. It was there that she met Will and Samantha Anderson who took her in and gave her shelter. The retirees had been traveling the country in a Winnebago motor home when they came upon the starving girl. Later, Maria could pinpoint the moment of her epiphany to a precise event.

———◆———

"When's the last time you ate or drank anything?" said Will, but Maria's eyes started to flutter and it appeared that she was fading into unconsciousness.

"Grab that water and those cheese and crackers from the table, Will. This will do until I can get a proper meal into her." After a few minutes of eating an entire sleeve of saltines and log of cheddar cheese, Maria seemed a new person and soon stood up.

"OK, shower or dinner first?" broke in Samantha in a matter of fact tone. Will playfully held his nose, displaying his preference. After Maria made her decision, Samantha selected some comfortable clothes from her wardrobe and hoped that the young woman would not be too put off by the "old-lady" outfit. Maria was thrilled to have something clean to wear.

"Poor girl," was all Will said, as she scampered off for a long overdue shower.

Dinner was some delicious hamburgers whose meat had been enhanced by Samantha's recipe of ingredients from her traveling spice rack. The fries and homemade coleslaw would have been enough food for the three of them, but Will insisted on throwing on two hot dogs just for good measure. Maria was so hungry that she would have eaten the entire cow that the meal had come from, yet she deferred from taking a hot dog.

"Don't like the dogs? They're all beef," injected Samantha knowing that they could have been all horsemeat and Maria still would have devoured them if something were not holding her back.

"There's only two. I don't want to take your portion." To this response, Will and Samantha both laughed heartily, and Maria looked puzzled.

"We weren't laughing at you. It's just that Sammie here won't eat hot dogs unless there's sauerkraut to put on them. And you don't find that very often west of the Mississippi." Though she took the hot dog, sadness seemed to envelop Maria.

"What is it girl?" questioned Samantha.

"My mom is the same way."

"Ah, I knew you were a New Yorker." Will laughed almost choking on a fry.

"Sauerkraut had nothing to do with that . . . I recognized the accent the first time you spoke," added Samantha. "We're from Brooklyn originally."

"Queens," answered Maria and proceeded to cover her hot dog with ketchup.

"Now that there is a downright mortal sin . . . ketchup on a dog? Are you kidding me?" scolded Will.

They finished the meal quietly, and Maria couldn't get up fast enough to help clean up after the feast. As she threw out the soiled paper plates and napkins, Samantha put away the condiments. Will started a campfire, and they were soon sitting around it and enjoying the peaceful feeling of pastel colored sunset.

"You haven't asked me anything about myself."

"If you want us to know, you'll tell us. If you don't, well then, it's none of our damn business." Maria didn't know if she was ready so she changed the subject.

"What about you two? What do you do?"

"This," answered Sam with a smile on her face. "Since we retired from teaching, we travel about in the Winnebago.

"All the time?"

"No," continued Will. "We take off for a few months at a time and travel around the country. In the last ten years, we have been in every state that our motorhome can reach. I won't drive to Alaska, and I can't drive to Hawaii. But we've seen the rest of them."

This harmless comment took the smile off of Maria's face.

"I've seen more of them than I wanted to . . . but no matter how far I travel I can't escape my thoughts." Will wanted to say something in answer to Maria's cry for help. Samantha gave him a gentle poke that silently told him, let her speak.

"Johnny's gone, and I don't know why." Maria put her hands to her face and started to cry uncontrollably. Samantha instinctively put her arm around her and Maria immediately clung to her. Maria's outburst was so filled with emotion that she had to gasp for air in between her sobs. After a few minutes, she seemed to gain control and looked into the faces of her two new friends. "Feelin' a little better?" said Will.

"That's the first time in over three years that I have said that out loud. It's really the first time since I left home that I had anyone to say it to."

"Don't you have people back home that you could have talked to?"

"No, my parents are part of the problem . . . and my friends are all dead."

"Dead? You can't be more than . . . what? . . . nineteen?"

"I'm twenty - two."

"Seems awfully young to have friends die?"

"It's a long story."

"Well, we've got nothing but time if you want to tell it . . . or I can get out my guitar, and we can sing around the campfire," said Will offering the young woman a choice for the direction of the rest of the night.

"Oh God, I don't care if you murdered ten people. Talk to us. Please, anything to stop him from taking out the guitar and singing!"

"Oh, c'mon, I'm not that bad," said Will defending himself, but with a smile that let Maria know that Samantha was probably telling the truth. A small grin formed on her face and her dour mood seemed to be broken. Maria didn't feel she was ready yet.

"I like music. I'd like to hear you play."

"I don't know if it qualifies as music. And don't be so sure that you want to hear Will play until you have sampled a bit of it," responded Sam. However, there was a smile on her face as she tenderly handed the guitar to her husband. "Sorry, Hon, I just had to warn her."

Maria thought that it was nice to be with good people and just enjoy music again. The night passed in mellow relaxation she had not felt in years. Late in the evening, Samantha's soft voice took over the singing duties, and Maria even joined in with her a few times on tunes that she remembered.

"Do you know this one?" said Will as he hit a familiar chord combination that the young girl recognized all too well— "Catch the Wind."

A gentle wind blew across the Arizona desert. Immediately, Maria was transported back to all the beauty and heartache of her former life. She remembered Johnny talking in song titles and likening them to philosophical statements.

"Me and you, Maria, we're going to catch that wind right out of this place," he would often say on hearing the song, or even at the slightest breeze that blew across their faces while they were together. "Always remember that." She had always been the skeptic. There was no getting out. Sure, her parents had moved to a neighborhood they thought was the Promised Land, but that had not changed their way of life, their closed minds, or their economic outlook. Johnny always thought beyond that.

"When the band makes it big, we'll get married right away."

"Johnny, you're such a dreamer," she would reply. Sure, things were looking great for the band that spring of 1967. However, that kind of success might not be permanent.

On a rare occasion, he revealed his serious side. "We will get out of here—no matter what it takes." It was then he surprised her with the fact that Queens College had accepted him. She had already sent in her deposit for the same school.

"If it ever looks like the band is not going to make it—and I do mean if—I'll be right there beside you at school and we'll make that future together, one way or another."

"Do you mean it, Johnny?" she had asked. "What about the music?"

"I love the music more than anything in this world— besides you. I promise you the future with me. I'll do whatever it takes."

"You OK?" Sam looked at despondent Maria.

"No," was the only reply. Samantha leaned over and again held her tight. Maria began to speak. She told them the story of her and Johnny.

Maria's life changed that night in the Arizona desert. She had gotten her thoughts and feelings together. Maria had no more tears left in her, but her forlorn look of loss was evident to both Will and Sam.

"Johnny always said that we would catch the wind and find our way."

"Maybe, you just weren't meant to do it together," answered Will.

"But he didn't even tell me he was leaving."

"Maybe he couldn't," responded Samantha softly.

"You mean because he was dead?"

"There are other choices, but that is one of them."

"Let's just say he wasn't a creep and leaving was not meant to hurt you."

"Johnny wasn't a creep."

"So there's your answer. Let's just say he couldn't tell you . . . or his leaving was better for you . . . or him . . . or both of you."

"Do you think that's true?"

"The question you have to ask yourself is a hard one. If he did it to save *your* life, then what have you done with that life?"

Maria had to stop and think about that statement. She understood so much now and she chastised herself for her time spent in self-pity.

The three of them talked long into the night as the campfire burned brightly. They spoke of her parents, her choices, and conflicts. They laughed and they cried as the night wore on. Maria's mind seemed to clear itself of all the clutter and distraction that had made her a lost soul for almost four years. As the morning light seemed to break the horizon and the fire had been reduced to a few dying embers, silence overtook the three of them. The quiet was broken by Maria's light-hearted question to the couple.

"And what about you two? What are you running from? You know, wandering out here in the wilderness?" Will and Sam laughed heartily.

"There is a phrase people like us use. Maybe someday it will catch on. You know, like on tee-shirts and bumper stickers. We always say, 'Not all those who wander are lost.' It's not original. It's from *The Hobbit*."

"I like that," said Maria with a slight chuckle. Will looked her in the eye and spoke to her more seriously than she expected.

"You see we always find our way home to our kids and grandkids. Yeah, we wander with no plan or purpose, but we are not lost. You, my dear girl, *are* lost."

"I guess I am . . . or was," Maria barely whispered.

"In fact, in a few days, we are heading home to New York. We wouldn't want to miss the twins' birthdays."

"How old?"

"Bella and Ava are two," replied Samantha. She then looked over at her husband and he nodded his approval to a question she had not even asked out loud.

"Do you want to come with us?"

"Yeah . . . I think that I'd like that."

It would take ten days to slowly wander across the country on their way home. They talked about many topics. Will and Sam shared their stories of teaching and retirement travels, and Maria filled in the details of her life. She spoke a great deal about Johnny and his band. She even talked extensively about her parents and her conflict with them. On the seventh day, she called home and told her mother and father that she was coming back.

Whether Johnny was dead or whether he had merely abandoned her, did not matter. She was ashamed of what she had done with *her* life. Johnny would not have wanted her to throw away everything because of him.

———•———

Slowly, Maria put the pieces of her existence back together. She had found her way home. She asked the forgiveness of her parents for the way that she had hurt them. She still argued constantly with them about many of the views they still held. This time, however, she dealt with them with considerably more patience and understanding. They loved her, even if they were a bit pig-headed. Much like the prodigal son in the Bible, the family reconciled upon her return. They would always disagree, but they could live with it.

———•———

In 1977, Maria graduated from Queens College. On her way to pick up her final paperwork necessary to participate in the actual ceremony, she had gotten into a minor fender bender near the school. The police officer who answered the call had been pleasant, not to mention good-looking. When he asked her out, she accepted. When they married in 1980, Maria had just turned 30. In the culture of the times, she bordered on being dubbed an old maid. She never felt that she had settled. She did love Jason Carlson. However, she knew in June of 1967 that she would never completely fall in love ever again. This was good enough, and she was happy.

Maria never saw Will and Samantha again, but she never forgot them. When she returned to college in January of 1972, she started taking courses toward becoming a teacher. It was a career that had been a possibility for her the first time she had attended Queens College. However, the tales of Will and Samantha inspired her to pursue the same field that these beloved friends had chosen.

Years later it did not surprise her husband Jason when she asked him if he thought William was a good name for their firstborn. They decided that the second child would be Sam whether it was a boy or a girl. Two years later, their daughter Samantha was born.

7

Journal of Johnny Cipp

Entry #96

"Listen to the Music"
- *The Doobie Brothers*

M Y BEST INTENTIONS WERE TO focus on the people I left behind and not on those who had died. Still, my mind keeps coming back to the band. Who did *they* leave behind when their lives were cut short? Not too many. There are no Brackowskis to remember Bracko. There are no Tinleys to remember Joey. I know now there are no Cippitellis to remember me. Perhaps, Gio's parents are still there. I will have to look into that. I don't know why it never occurred to me before that besides Jimmy Mac, everyone in the band had no siblings. Perhaps that is what bound us together so tightly.

The Music Doctor haunts me. As much as I want to move on, songs keep running through my consciousness, and every one of them is tied to the guys. I think the Doctor is a sadist at times. As I was driving out here to take my walk,

"Fire" by The Crazy World of Arthur Brown came on the radio. Really?

Fire, to destroy all you've done.
Fire, to destroy all you've become.

Was the goddamn Music Doctor sitting at Bracko's house two decades ago when he died? Was he there when the flames consumed his life besides all his dreams—*all he'd become, all he'd done*? I promised myself not to dwell on these thoughts that have controlled me for so long.

I would give anything just to hear the band play again. I know that sounds crazy (something new?). I can almost hear the tapes we teased Jimmy Mac about. They are playing in my head. Perhaps, Jimmy's mom and three sisters are enjoying them on the old recorder that he used to religiously tape our practices. Maybe, it just hurt too much, and Mrs. Mac destroyed them. I just don't know, but it was all I thought of as I walked today.

I almost can hear Jimmy Mac harping on us not to start playing until the machine was recording.

———◆———

"Johnny, wait! The tape isn't running yet?"

"Hey, Jimmy Mac, you got a side business selling bootleg versions of our music," teased Gio.

"Not high enough quality to sell," interrupted Joey.

"Tinman, I was kidding. Absolutely no sense of humor on you. You're so tight, your ass squeaks."

"Oh . . . OK," said a satisfied Joey Tinman.

"Jimmy Mac, you're not . . .?" questioned Gio.

"Not what?" said the now distracted Jimmy Mac.

"Selling them?"

"Fuck off, Gio," said Jimmy Mac pressing the record button.
"What's my cut of the sales?"
Bracko hit a loud resounding chord and started to play the song
"Money."

———◆———

I remember laughing when private conversations were caught on the tapes. Some of these were never meant for consumption by the public. Sometime in April of our last year, our resident songwriter and my friend, DJ Spinelli came by to help us with one of the songs I had written with him.

"DJ fuckin' Spinelli, what the hell are you staring at?"
"Nothing, Jimmy Mac, nothing."
"Now you're calling my sister Aylin's ass nothing?"
"Er, no, I mean I wasn't looking at nothing," said the stuttering DJ Spinelli.
"Anything," interrupted Tinman.
"What?" said both DJ and Jimmy Mac in unison.
"I wasn't looking at nothing' is a double negative. You're sup-posed say, 'I wasn't looking at anything'."
"Shut the fuck up, Tinman. He's looking at my kid sister's ass, and you're giving us a lesson in grammar?"
"You're right, Joey. If I intend to make a career of writing, I must be more careful."
"Shut the fuck up. My little sister's honor is at stake, and you two nerds are still talking grammar."
Bracko started to play the notes to the song "Words" by the Bee Gees. And the entire band paused to look in his direction. The argument was over.

I wonder if DJ ever did tell Aylin of his interest. She was

only a year and a half younger than him, and he did confess to me in school one day that he had a thing for her. (I never told Jimmy Mac that part.)

Where are those tapes now? Our hearts and souls are embedded in them. They are the only tangible remnant of our existence. I would give anything just to hear a vocal by Jimmy Mac and Gio. Or a Tinman solo on the organ. Or just one note from Bracko's guitar.

There are golden moments on those tapes—wherever they are today.

8

Time Passages:
"Listen to the Music"
– The Doobies Brothers

AFTER THE MURDER OF HER husband and son, life for Adele McAvoy and her three daughters became a struggle to exist. She could no longer keep the family business going. Her only solace came during her moments listening to "the tape."

Adele's brother James had been a building super in the city. When one of his tenants had skipped town in the middle of the night, he had the job of emptying the apartment. Among the piles of junk left behind, James found cases of blank cassette tapes. Having no use for them, he gave them to his namesake nephew, Jimmy Mac. In turn, the drummer used the tapes to record every moment of practice that the band had during its last year. With an unlimited tape supply, the young drummer became careless about turning the recorder on and off.

Months after the deaths of her husband and son, Adele got up the nerve to try and clean out the basement. There she came upon the forgotten recorder. For no logical reason, she pressed play.

———◆———

"August 15, 1967. OK, got my drums back today from the police. Think I'll get in a little practice. It won't be the same with-out the guys. But who knows? Maybe we'll get back together when this whole thing blows over. Well, if we can—without Bracko . . . (unsteady voice of Jimmy Mac interrupted by footsteps coming downstairs)

"Dad, can you see if I pressed record on the tape player?" (Jimmy Mac)

"Yup, you did. Hey, listen you don't have long to practice on those things. We have to go relieve your mom at the store." (Noel McAvoy)

"Oh my God," cried Adele upon hearing the voice of her beloved husband. She realized that this was recorded on the last day of his life. She realized that they had barely seen each other as they exchanged places at the candy store. This was the last conversation that Noel and Jimmy Mac had had at home.

"How are you doing?" (Noel)
"OK, I guess . . . maybe." (Jimmy Mac)"
"You just gotta push through the best you can." (Noel)
"I'll try." (Jimmy Mac)
"You know what works for me? Love. When things go bad, the love of good people gets you through." (Noel)
"Really?" (Jimmy Mac)
"Really, Jimmy, I can see it working in you right now."
"Me?"
"I see the way you look when Diane is around."
"D-a-a-a-d!"
"Jimmy, you hold onto that feeling as long as you can. I have the

love of the greatest woman in the whole wide world, and I wouldn't trade it for anything. I cherish your mother that much. Think about it. Diane will help you. OK, remember, ten minutes then we have to go."

Adele cried through the ten remaining minutes of the ear-splitting drum solo that followed on the tape. She continued to replay that final conversation for the rest of her life.

9

Journal of Johnny Cipp

Entry # 97

"I-Feel-Like-I'm-Fixin'-To-Die-Rag"
- *Country Joe and the Fish*

HERE IT IS 1990, AND I suddenly have a weird flash-back to thoughts I had long forgotten. I know that I am safe now but for a decade of my life, I was a wanted man, and I don't mean by that murdering sack of shit, Guy Provenzano.

Having turned 18 in late June of 1967, I was then a criminal. With the war in Vietnam raging, I was required to register for the draft. I hadn't done so because I was busy hiding from the Provenzano family and later working on a cotton farm under an assumed name. I don't think that the Selective Service lists this as grounds for a deferment. There is no 4M — *deferred by reason hiding from a death-wishing maniac.*

In truth, I always wondered how my life would have played out if I hadn't had to run. Would I have been drafted? Would the record company have found some way of getting me a deferment? Maybe I would join the National Guard with the only downside being a permanent haircut that was decidedly un-rock and roll.

I had nothing against the military. I loved the music that was *against* the war because it was creative. Pro-war music was limited to Barry Sadler's "Ballad of the Green Berets." Anti-war stuff flooded the charts. However, I was nonpolitical. In the end, my anti-draft stance came down to the fact that I was more afraid of dying in the jungles of New York than I was of dying in those of Southeast Asia. The Viet Cong were only vague enemies in my mind. On the other hand, Mad Guy Provenzano and his schoolyard lynching had been real to me. And so I never looked back, and I never thought about the desires of the United States government and the rules of the Selective Service. As a result, I would soon come to realize that I could never go home. I know that President Jimmy Carter eventually pardoned all those who ran away from the draft, but by then I cared about nothing. I knew nothing of the world around me.

I still have never voted. I mean, how can I? Officially I don't exist. I can't help but think of the irony of the whole situation. Guy Provenzano had murdered at least ten people that I know of, yet I was the one who was a fugitive from the law.

———◆———

My walk extended a bit longer today as I pondered just what had happened to the bad guys. I realized now no one had found me. Why not? Had I been that good at hiding my tracks while fleeing like a coward? Or had the myth that there were only four members of Those Born Free held up? Maybe I have been hiding all these years for no reason? Maybe no one had been looking for me all this time.

Wouldn't that be a kick in the ass if I threw my life away for nothing?

I now know that my mother and father died of natural causes in the seventies. But what of Gio's parents? Had Mad Guy been content with the death of their son and the cover story that he ran away? Or had his desperate insanity known no limits of time?

Had Guy and his gang ever been accused of all the crimes they perpetrated? Or had madman mellowed, settled down into a nice straight life inclusive of a sweet wife and that suburban life I so often fantasize about? Wouldn't that be a load of crap? All the good people are dead or suffering while evil lives in a house with a white picket fence?

10

Time Passages:
"Bad to the Bone"
– George Thorogood and the Delaware Destroyers

FOR THE CIPPITELLI AND DEANGELIS families, there would always remain a deep and abiding sadness in their lives. They still held out hope that someday they would be reunited with their sons. For the Cippitelli family, this *would* not happen. For the DeAngelis family, it *could* not happen. The rise and fall of Those Born Free had affected many lives. None of the members of the band would ever know how much impact they had had on this world. As time passed, the brokenhearted and insane alike started to move on with their lives.

October 1967

Detective Richard Shea had been assigned to investigate two missing young persons: Giovanni DeAngelis and John Cippitelli. To any honest police officer, the choice of Shea made absolutely no sense at all. Homicide detectives did *not* work missing persons' cases. It was already a bit out of line when Shea had been given the nod to pursue the facts concerning the deaths of Stanley and Rocco Brackowski. If their deaths had *not* been an accident, then this was a case for the arson squad. Shea already had his hands full trying to track down the thugs who had murdered the victims in the McAvoy case. A missing person's case placed in his lap made no sense at all unless you understood who was pulling the strings. Most cops knew the score even if they weren't playing the game.

———◆———

The tall, pale officer approached the door of the DeAngelis home and knocked aggressively on the glass panes of the aluminum storm door. When Rosalie DeAngelis answered, he introduced himself and stated his purpose.

"Good afternoon, Mrs. DeAngelis. Could I have a moment of your time? I am Detective Richard Shea." Mr. and Mrs. De Angelis believed the police department would pay little attention to an apparent runaway case. Still, remarkably, here was a young detective standing at their door. While there, he studied the note left behind by Gio and made a perfunctory statement about never giving up on finding the boy. In reality, the case was now closed. He did not need any more information. He had all *he* needed to know. As he exited the house, he turned to Gyp and Rosalie DeAngelis and asked one final question.

"Did you know that another boy has gone missing?"

"Oh, you mean Johnny . . . Johnny Cippitelli?" replied Gyp DeAngelis.

"Yeah, that's the name. Did Gio know him?"

"Did he know him? They have been best friends for ten years."

"Any chance that they left together?"

"They did everything together. Stickball, TV, and . . . of course, the band."

"The band?" Shea acted surprised, but he knew just where this conversation was going to lead.

"Yeah, until four months ago, those two spent every minute of their free time playing in a group called Those Born Free. I guess when that fell apart, they decided to take off and start a new band somewhere. I think that they were both upset, you know, those guys all dying." Gyp DeAngelis stopped and thought for a second, and then looked down at the business card that the detective had slipped in his hand upon his arrival. He had forgotten that he even held it. *Detective Richard Shea, Homicide Investigations.*

"You don't think?"

"No, no. According to all our facts that just doesn't seem likely." With that, he gave a reassuring handshake to the now confused father and finally said, "Don't worry a bit. He'll turn up."

"Just let me know if I can help at all," offered the desperate father.

"In fact, there is something that you can do. Do you have any pictures of your son and this Johnny Cippitelli?" Gyp DeAngelis quickly went into his son's room and a few minutes later returned with a picture of the entire band.

"That's my son on the right, and that's Johnny . . . the one he's leaning his elbow on."

"Thanks, this will help a great deal," replied the detective as he got up to leave. Richie Shea had many more stops to make that day. He would report to the precinct to explain to his captain what he had found out. He then would speak to his *real* boss so that he could determine how to handle the interview with the Cippitelli family. He was very proud of his day's work so far.

The next day, Detective Shea visited the Cippitelli home. He had spent the night deciding how to act toward Johnny's parents. Gone was the sympathetic cop that had been to the

DeAngelis home. While questioning Gio's parents, he had *known* what had happened to their son. However, when he dealt with Johnny's parents, he needed some firm information. This kid was not missing but rather on the run, and he needed to know where he had gone. He knocked firmly on the wooden door announcing the no-nonsense attitude of his visit. Ushered in by Mr. and Mrs. Cippitelli, he refused all pleasantries. No coffee, no tea, and no smiles were to be the rule of the day.

"So how long had your son and the DeAngelis boy been at odds?" Shea had preplanned his attack specifically to catch Johnny's parents off guard. "How long do you think that your son was planning his revenge against Gio?"

"What the fuck?" was the only response from the blind-sided John Cippitelli, Sr.

"John, watch your language," whispered his equally flummoxed wife, Anna.

"I mean the kid throws your son out of the band, and then he steals his girl. Of course, Johnny would lose his temper," probed the detective. However, his attempt to fluster the older man with these accusations had confused the whole issue. Shea lay back for a moment. He realized he had too many unsubstantiated statements. John Cippitelli looked at him in total puzzlement.

"What is he talking about?" injected Anna into the conversation, yet both men seemed to be waiting for the other to make the first move. Shea blinked first.

"Well, that's what I have been told," mumbled the detective realizing that he had overplayed his hand.

"Oh yeah, who told you that?"

"I'm not at liberty to reveal my sources," continued the now defensive investigator.

"Well, I'm not at liberty to allow you to stay in my house and shovel bullshit. So get your fucking ass out of my sight."

He turned to his wife and spoke softly, "Sorry for the language."

"I'm just trying to do my job, Mr. Cippitelli. You've got to understand."

"If this is doing your job, kid, you better find a new line of work," howled Cippitelli, using all his powers of restraint not to throw in any more off-color words in front of his wife. Seeing the cop duly put in his place, he walked to the door and opened it. The message was clear. *Leave.* However, as if to justify his anger and attitude, he felt that he had to state his case. "My son and Gio were best buddies until the day they both went missing. I guess that they are together somewhere trying to start all over with a new band that will be just as good as the old one. You see that whole 'out of the band story' was old news. They were playing together until the very end."

"Thank you for the help, Mr. Cippitelli," said Shea pleasantly as he worked his way through the proffered open door. He meant it. With his last barb, he had a second confirmation of Johnny as the fifth member of the group. Richie Shea smoothed his pale fingers through his red wavy hair. In every aspect of his physical appearance, he looked the like a true son of Ireland, the country where his father had been born. Very few people saw any resemblance to his mother, Theresa Ingoglia. Therefore, no one ever made the connection to Theresa's sister, Carmela, her husband, Dominick Provenzano, or his first cousin, Guy Provenzano.

"Madman Across the Water"
- Elton John

1967

Guy Provenzano continued with his life. He would never give up the hatred he felt for those who had destroyed his ambitions. They had robbed him of any chance of ever being a *capo*. He had been assured that he could reach *some* level of success in the organization. However, they did not have to tell him outright that he was not the leader that he had pictured himself to be. His rise to success had been and would be severely be limited.

He would find and kill Johnny Cipp. His cousin Richie had confirmed that the runaway had been a part of the band that had brought about his downfall. He would never forget. He would never give up the search. And after Cipp's death, he would then go back and revisit the families and friends of those bastards who had cut his balls off. Yes, first Johnny Cipp and then more. This he vowed to himself.

1967 – 1984

Time passed, and the memory of Those Born Free faded. The Provenzanos no longer lived in the Heights. In the crime family's view, that neighborhood was now a barren wasteland, populated by drug-addled *moulies*. It mattered little that they had been responsible for much of the carnage that had befallen the area.

By the time he hit thirty, Guy, his wife, and their two young boys lived outside of the city limits. They were very comfortable in a Manhasset estate that boasted a long, elaborate entranceway complete with stone statues of lions at the driveway gates. Despite not reaching the success that he had hoped for, Guy could now afford to move to Nassau County's North Shore; the Gold Coast made famous by *The Great Gatsby*. The Provenzano family had had its roots in the area of Kent Avenue in Brooklyn before the generational stop-over in Cambria Heights. They had come a long way from the tenement building in which Guy and Tony had been born. The North Shore would be a perfect place to raise his family. None of *those* people lived here.

He should have been happy, but he was not. Nearing his fortieth birthday, Guy had become a very bitter, angry man. He only had contact with his superiors when they required it. His hopes of moving up in the organization had been dashed because of the debacle of the Driftwood and his failure to control his fury after that. In total, his rampage of revenge had notched eleven holes of death on his belt. He had thought himself very subtle in his executions. However, it had taken substantial influence with the police to keep him from being implicated in the holocaust in the Heights. He had not been subtle enough to the powers above him. Guy had become an outcast with the very people he had once hoped to impress.

It was very likely that he would have remained a lower level thug had it not been for his father's early-onset dementia. While still in his 50's, Dom Provenzano had started to lose his faculties. At first, it was just a forgotten name or appointment. However, before long his reduced capacities had thrown the entire organization into confusion. Guy could not stand by and watch their kingdom to slip away. He would not let his father's fragile state embarrass him. To keep this from happening, Guy took over day-to-day control of their small empire. The vast potential wealth of the suburban county of Nassau had been taken off the table two decades ago, and Guy never forgot the reasons why.

He had deceived the entire organization for three years before the elder Provenzano's disability became impossible to hide. Guy had chosen to put his father in a home rather than deal with the nauseating sight of the old man.

His mother had protested. However, Guy no longer listened to what she had to say. Also, when he threatened to have his brother committed too if she opened her mouth again, Carmela had backed down.

Guy now had to face the family bosses and try to keep control of his fortunes. He even considered a first strike salvo but did not think he had the firepower. In the end, he had been pleasantly surprised. They had admired how well he had run the business during his father's illness. Ironically, his three-year deception had garnered him more bravos. Therefore, "Mad Guy" Provenzano had taken over the throne of his father's kingdom.

"Birthday"
- The Beatles

1984

"Where're you going?" said the surprised Christina Provenzano as her husband Guy put on his overcoat and started toward the front door of their house.

"Out," was the abrupt answer from the sullen Mad Guy.

He didn't owe her any explanation. She was quite a looker, had a body to die for, and the sex was quite exceptional. It had produced two young sons to carry on the Provenzano dynasty. However, she got a great deal in return. He gave her a beautiful house, clothes, cars . . .anything material that she wanted. Love? Mad Guy had long ago realized that he could not, would not love anyone or anything. In fact, he even denied that love was an actual reality in this world. He understood hate, fear, cruelty, and a whole host of other negative feelings that satisfied him and helped him get along in life. But love? What did that ever do for you?

"Don't forget that your Mom and brother are coming over for the cake later? It's not every day you turn forty."

"What time does that whole bullshit start?" Mad Guy had no intention of being there on time. If he felt generous, he would show up at the last possible moment just to appease his Mom. If he felt anything for anyone in this world, it was his mother. Or maybe it was just the fact that she still had control over some of Provenzano family wealth. He really didn't know or care.

And then there was Tony. They had been a great team as kids and teenagers. Then the stupid bastard had wrecked his brain huffing glue. Now he was a worthless piece of shit. Yet, for some reason, he still hung out with the imbecile. His mom always asked Guy to take care of Tony when she went for an extended stay to visit dear old demented dad. On those occasions, Guy's wife Christina treated Tony like her third son and baked for him and played childish games that were suited for their two young children Carmine and Dominick, but seemed ridiculous for the thirty-seven-year-old Tony.

Occasionally, Guy took his brother out on his boat. Most of the time this was to appease his mother. Tony never said a word. He just stared out into the vast waters of the Long Island Sound and felt the wind blow through his hair as his brother sped through the waters that separated Connecticut from Long Island.

There would be no boat today. There would be no one joining Mad Guy for today's activities. It was his fortieth birthday, and he was going to provide his own present. After all, you only turn forty once. Guy's idea of a good time did not include cake or dimwitted relatives. No, for your fortieth birthday you should treat yourself to something you will really enjoy. Something you really want to do.

Guy's Cadillac entered the Long Island Expressway just as

the autumn sun lay on the horizon. Almost blinded by the glaring light, he made his way to exit 30 and the ramp to the Cross Island Parkway. By then the sun had set, and he had to put on his lights in order to find the exit onto Linden Boulevard. He traveled westward on this thoroughfare until he reached 222nd Street. He turned off the headlights of his car and drove in the darkness until he reached 116th Avenue. It had been years since he had last driven these streets. That had been a time when he and his brother had ruled this kingdom. He cared not. He had moved on. Still, one bit of business remained to be taken care of in the Heights. No, not business. This was pleasure. This was his gift to himself. He was going to do something he had wanted to do for a long time.

With its lights out, the Cadillac stopped in front of the third house from the corner. He exited the car. He pulled the collar of his coat up as both a protection against the biting cold and the prying eyes of nosy neighbors. He walked up to the door and knocked.

When a gray-haired woman in her sixties answered the door, she hesitated opening it to the stranger.

"How can I help you?"

"I need to speak to you," said Guy softly.

"Gyp, there is someone at the door. Should I open it?"

"Find out what he wants before you unlock the storm door," yelled Gyp DeAngelis from deep in the house. Rosalie pulled back. However, Mad Guy Provenzano knew precisely the words needed to get inside the house.

"I have news about your son, Gio."

She opened the door rapidly and allowed the madman into her house. As Gyp entered the room from the kitchen, he saw his wife talking to a stranger . . . no, not a stranger. It was starting to dawn on him exactly who was in his house, but he was too late. He heard his wife speak her final words

. . . ever.

"So, what happened to Gio?"

"I killed him seventeen years ago," said the madman and he drew his KSC Glock with the 150mm silencer and shot her in the middle of the forehead.

He expected Gyp DeAngelis to attack him but instead was amused when the man threw himself on the floor to be with his wife.

"Interesting choice for your last moment of life," commented the amused murderer. Gyp did not answer. He merely cried over the body of his wife. Finally, he looked up and simply said, "Why?"

"It's been a long time coming for me to finish this story."

"Story?"

"Yeah, I let you live so no one would suspect that I had strangled your son."

Gyp DeAngelis rose quickly from his wife's body and sprang at Provenzano faster than a man his age should have been able to move. His hands almost reached the neck of the madman when the Glock again fired into the forehead of its second victim. Gyp DeAngelis died immediately.

Mad Guy quickly exited the DeAngelis house. In the darkness, he entered his car and drove away, all the while singing softly to himself,

Happy Birthday to me,
Happy Birthday to me,
Happy Birthday, dear Mad Guy,
Happy Birthday to me.

11

Journal of Johnny Cipp

Entry # 98

"Sad Little Girl"
- *The Beau Brummels*

MY JOURNAL NEVER LIES TO me. As I reread through the worn and water-stained pages, I see patterns. There are patterns of love and loyalty. And ambition and anguish. Contemplation and confusion. Creation and destruction. Fun and failure. My failures—my many, many failures. I think I have come to understand all of them except for my failure to Riet.

Who was she? Or rather who *is* she? Where *is* she? What the hell is her real name? I know Gio only referred to her as 'Riot,' reminding me of the explosive nature of their relationship. However, I once caught Gio writing a note addressed to R–i–e–t, so I knew how she spelled it. Was that her real name? A nickname? Short for something? What?

I am only stalling the inevitable. I don't want to face the reality of her life. Was she hurt as much as I think Maria was hurt? Was there genuinely love between Gio and Riet? Wait a minute, am I racist? Did I feel that their relationship was somehow less valid than that of Maria and me? Is it because they were from the two different worlds of the Heights? What an ass I've been. I loved Maria, and I just ran. How big a shithead am I being? I'm questioning Gio's commitment to her. Who the fuck do I think I am? He died trying to get to her one last time. Not me. Perhaps that is the guilt that plagues me most. I couldn't do that one little thing for him. Was it because I knew nothing about her? Did I dismiss her because she was not my friend? Or because she was black? But the new me is not supposed to worry about myself. I told myself that I would think about those I hurt and what had become of their lives.

How can I know anything about her? How long did she mourn his loss never knowing that he had died? When did she finally let go? Did she ever forget him?

12

Time Passages:
"Sad Little Girl"
– The Beau Brummels

October 1967

RIET LIVED MOST OF THE rest of her life never knowing why the man she had loved had left. Usually,
"white" rumors did not filter down to the black community. Riet, therefore, made an effort to track down the
one persistent bit of information that had surfaced—Gio
was gone.

The Carvel store where Gio and Riet had met over a year
before would soon be closing for the winter months. Not
many people would be walking up to the window to pur-
chase their patented brown bonnets or flying saucers as the
weather grew cold. Knowing that this was the one place
where the employer and employees would comprehend that
this black girl knew this particular white boy, she casually
appeared one day on the pretense of visiting her former
colleagues. After a painfully long period of small talk, she
brought the conversation around to Gio.

"What happened to Ned and . . . what was that white kid's

name, Gippy or something like that?" It was a shallow cover up to her real intentions of finding out what had happened to Gio without letting on that they had been together since meeting there as co-workers.

"Who?" responded Walt Kimski, a white man who did not care about the race of his employees as long as they worked long and hard. Though his employees genuinely liked the man, they often joked that he did not see black and white, but rather only green.

"You mean that white boy, Gio?" offered Sally Jenkins, a young black girl who had continued to work for Kimski since the summer before. Riet often thought that Sally had taken a liking to Gio herself and might have made a move if Gio had not suddenly quit that summer to pursue the band.

"Yeah, ah, him and Ned." throwing the black boy's name back into the conversation just for appearances. In reality, Ned and Gio had almost come to blows while working together. Ned seemed to have eyes for Riet himself and might have noticed the fact that something was going on between Gio and her. Words were said, and the situation might have escalated if they both had not needed their jobs. Kimski had explained unequivocally that he would not tolerate any violence from his workers.

"Well, ya know, sister, that Ned's gone. I mean gone as in up the river, in the clink, doing time," laughed Sally. "That temper finally got the best of him." A long silence followed. Riet was determined not to give away her interest by asking specifically about her boyfriend. Kimski and Sally went about the task of doing the season-ending cleanup and seemed to have lost track of the fact that Riet stood staring at them. Finally, Kimski turned to the young black girl. His eyes took on a much kinder expression than he usually displayed to the younger generation. He approached her and gently placed one arm around her shoulder guiding her away from the work area occupied by Sally.

"He's gone. Ran away from home. Left a note that broke his parents' hearts. No one has any idea where he went." He then looked into her eyes with an expression that implied a genuine feeling for her unspoken loss. "You'll be OK."

She smiled gratefully at him and headed for the door. He gave her a wave that conveyed understanding and sympathy. *He knew about us,* thought Riet as she exited.

Riet never found out what happened to Gio. She lived her life as best she could. It would never be easy for her. Yet, in her heart, she knew he had not simply abandoned her. She never lost the feeling that she loved Gio and he loved her.

13

Journal of Johnny Cipp

Entry #99

"See My Friends"
- *The Kinks*

IT IS LATE FEBRUARY 1990, and I think this journal is coming to an end. I always promised myself when I started catching up with current times, it would then be time to tuck this baby away in a drawer somewhere. I only continued it this far because Padre suggested I write more after my . . . um. . . almost fatal swim. I have gone through my past incessantly, and I now look to the future. To do what? I don't exactly know. I have written about everyone, and I have thought about everyone. Starting next week, my thoughts will be of the future. Unless something comes up, I am done. I'm going to use this final entry to tighten up some loose ends. Though I have no answers, I do have questions.

I have mentioned before that I always wondered about Brother Christian. He was such a misfit in the rigid Catho-

lic school of Bishop McCarthy. He changed everything that
happened in my life by teaching me to play the bass. Is that
a good thing or a bad thing? But where is he now?

DJ Spinelli was the closest friend that I had outside the
band and the Heights. We shared many feelings and writings through my tough times. The last time I talked to him,
he was going to start Queens College. Did he ever run into
Maria there? I know he ended up being the writer he always
dreamed of being. I have seen his byline on magazines and
newspapers all through the years. Always writing about
music. At least he's keeping the faith. How I wish I could
see him again.

And then there is Tony. He was so many things to me—
bad and good. But in the end, he was a friend. I can see that
beaming smile as the band played at practice, or when he
danced with Maria, or when I played the ridiculous song
for him in the Garden of Eden. Does he smile anymore?
All of us are gone now, and Tony is trapped in a world surrounded by a criminal father and a psychotic brother. Has
he survived?

14

Time Passages:
"The Loner"
– Neil Young

1967 to 1990

BY THE TIME HE HIT his late thirties, Tony Provenzano had ceased to function in society. His only human interaction took place with his mother, and on a rare occasion, with his brother. He had withdrawn into a shell that revolved around watching infantile cartoons and eating his mother's pasta. Occasionally, his brother would take him out on his boat. Tony liked the calm and solitude that the ocean gave to him.

It had not always been like this. For years, Tony had clung to the moments of happiness he found in the dark recesses of his damaged brain. He could not remember the times that he had spent being the tough younger Provenzano brother. He could not remember intimidating all who crossed his path. Thankfully, those memories had disappeared after that tragic night. In fact, very few memories of the first four decades of his life survived in his thoughts. Frequently, he struggled hard to remember where he was. However, Tony did have some memories, and they all were of the happiest time of his life. He could not remember many of the details, but he smiled when he thought of Johnny, Gio, Bracko, Joey Tinman, and Jimmy Mac. Their faces had rapidly faded from memory, but still, he remembered being happy.

Tony knew nothing of death or disappearance. Throughout the late summer and early fall of 1967, the younger Provenzano brother had continued to show up every afternoon at the Garden of Eden. He spent the ensuing hours waiting for either Bracko or Johnny. He knew that if they showed up the music would begin and he would smile and laugh. He knew that they might be practicing with Gio, Jimmy, and Joey. He could never remember the name. Was it the Birthday Boys? That didn't sound right. Freedom Babies, no that was silly. He even had trouble remembering where Jimmy Mac's house was located so that he could use his open invitation to their practices. And so he went and sat in the Garden of Eden every day.

But no one ever came. Tony sat as the cold weather took the leaves from the bushes and bared his presence to those who looked into the garden and laughed at him. He sat as the winter winds lowered temperatures to levels deemed unbearable to most human beings. Still no one came. Soon he could not even remember why he sat and waited each day. Eventually the Provenzanos moved from the Heights and Tony went with them. He soon forgot the small overgrown section of the park. He could not remember the Heights. He could not remember the name Those Born Free. However, he never forgot that there were once five people who had played their music and had taken him into their hearts.

PART
3

"Turn the Page"
- Bob Seger and the Silver Bullet Band

15

Journal of Johnny Cipp

Entry #100

"Synchronicity"
- *The Police*

BESIDES THE POLICE SONG OF the same name, I always liked the word *synchronicity*, the coming together of individual events at a precise moment in time that results in something special. I might've gone forever with my laid-back life in Key West if it hadn't been for a coming together of people and events a few days ago. Maybe this is it. Maybe this will lead to me doing something really good. Maybe this is the first step on my path to redemption. What do you think, Music Doctor? When I get things right, will you let me know with just the right song? What will that song be? What will be the words and music that tell me I have done well?

What will be the sound of my redemption?

I thought I had finished writing in this journal last week. A sure sign of this is that I was starting to write some of my entries in the present tense. So I stopped writing. My last journal entry was a week ago and so much changed last Monday that I decided I needed to chronicle the events as they happened. Just for one more week.

By last Monday, my runs had become real workouts. I averaged two miles every other day and was feeling real changes in my physical condition. After my warm-up walk, I began seriously running along the highway. I passed the many businesses of Cudjoe Key and was actually starting to get my first taste of the effect known as a "runner's high." Still a high, but a much healthier one.

This was peak tourist season and the snowbirds had found their way even to these outlying areas of Key West. More than once, I had to alter my running path to avoid getting run over by a vacationing driver. I reached my turnaround point of mile marker 21 in good shape and began the return trip to mile marker 20.

Synchronicity. That morning was a moment that defined the word. As I re-approached the Bow Channel Bridge, one of those tourists mentioned above almost took my life. Distracted by the dazzling view of the sunlight glistening on the water, the driver lost concentration and veered toward me. Trapped between the moving vehicle and the deep blue sea, I saw my life pass before my eyes faster than it ever had in this journal. Inches away from crushing me against the concrete railing, he corrected his path and just barely missed me.

Now it was my turn to lose concentration. Obsessing over my near-death experience, I unconsciously continued to run past my car. As I passed the mile marker sign that lay outside of Mangrove Mama's, I came into a stretch of road that reflected where this famous restaurant had gotten its name. As far as I could see, the mangrove trees dominated the side of the road to the point where nothing else was visible. Coming to my senses, I took this as a sign that perhaps I would stretch my run a bit longer that day. No logic in that decision, just synchronicity. At Crane Avenue, I would view the Sugarloaf School. There I would turn back east toward my waiting car. It would make my total run three miles, quite an accomplishment.

Overambitious is another word that comes to mind when I think back. As I approached the intersection, I realized I had bitten off more than I could chew. I was exhausted beyond comprehension and found myself with two choices. I could push on and then rest at the school, or I could give up now and crawl back to my car.

Synchronicity. I made my decision. I decided to stop only after I had reached the school. It was then that I heard sounds I remembered well: the familiar crack of the bat, the slap of a ball tucking itself into the pocket of a leather glove, the voices of players excited to be playing the game. These were the sounds of baseball. As I cleared that last grove of trees that bordered the road, the field came into sight and with it a group of college-age players. But it wasn't so much the players that caught my attention, but rather their coach, a very familiar face. Everything changed that day . . . everything.

Synchronicity.

Entry #101

"Take Me Out to The Ballgame"
- *Jack Norworth*

Sugarloaf School houses kindergarten to eighth-grade students. Because of the constant threat of hurricanes, its sea green walls displayed very few windows. The largest wall of the building was the exterior gymnasium support that rose an imposing hundred feet above an adjoining baseball field. It formed an impressive end to the playing area in right field. I would learn later that the players now practicing on the field had dubbed it the "sea green monster," a reference to its being a pale version of the famous Green Monster in Boston's Fenway Park.

The players on the fields of Sugarloaf School obviously weren't students of the school itself, which might hold some 14-year-olds as its elder statesmen. The younger faces gazed at the older players as their gym teacher pointed out the nuances of the game of baseball.

Still, I wondered what these older players were doing there? By the time I reached the fencing that separated the field from the road, I couldn't run a step further. That athlete of the 1960s had long since left the building. Still the practice brought back such proud memories.

My mistreatment after my injury had turned me bitter for so long that I had forgotten the beauty of the game. However, watching these young players, I found myself drifting away into thoughts of what might have been. A security guard abruptly woke me from my daydream. He had been observing me, an unkempt, smelly letch, watching these young men play. He thought I might be a pervert who had lecherous desires for elementary school kids who lined the outside of the field. His minimum qualification for the job didn't stop him from having visions of being a hero who would save these kids from my clutches. As I tried to explain I'd been jogging, I could see him assessing my appearance. Could anyone actually be exercising in this heat? He seemed only moments away from calling for professional backup to rid the school of my threat.

"He's with me," I heard a familiar voice say and turned to see Cal interrupting my imminent arrest. As I mentioned before, Cal is my AA sponsor and has been a large part of my recovery. He has guided me through difficult times and talked me through many a rough night. Yet, I knew nothing about his real life. That's the way it's supposed to be in AA. From both his manner and his dress, I realized he was in charge of this whole practice. This caught me by surprise. While I'd told him some of the decisions in my life had been flavored by my bitterness about my baseball career, he never mentioned he could relate first-hand to my feelings.

I would later find out that he had been through what I had been through; only his experiences had been at the professional level. After I had spoken to the group at the meetings of AA a few times, he had approached me. I hadn't known until now why he had picked me. I also understood why he found my analogy of "two strikes" as a mentor the week before to be so interesting.

As the frustrated security guard shuffled away, I could see the loss in his eyes. I would have been his first big "collar." Cal looked at me and made some remark about me being all sweaty and smelly, and joked that I *should* have been carted away just for that. Anticipating my first question, he said, "I'm their coach."

We walked toward the field, and Cal explained. In his civilian life, Cal was the coach of a South Florida college team. As a team, they were doing OK, but he needed to get them away from the distractions of the mainland. He had arranged for the players to stay down here in the Lower Keys during their school break. Away from the hustle and bustle of campus life, they would practice the fundamentals. They needed an escape from the press who tended to pick apart every team in the baseball-crazed areas of Florida.

This explanation still left me a bit confused. How could I know Cal so well all the way down in Key West while he was busy coaching a team in the Miami area? The explanation he provided was logical. Cal had purposely kept his two lives separate. He lived in the town of Marathon, a location halfway between Miami and Key West. He traveled 50 miles up to his job and 50 miles down to Key West for his other life as a recovering alcoholic. This way his two worlds would never intersect. That is, until now. I'd been the one to bring these diverse parts of his life together.

We talked for a while mostly about baseball and for the first time I got to know Cal as a person. He cared about these kids and this program. It was a minor Division I school that only succeeded because Cal could recruit from some very rough areas around the country. In those locations, he convinced young athletes they could escape their turbulent lives through his program. As a black man and former major league player, he had credibility with these kinds of kids that most white coaches did not. More importantly, he had a reputation of coming through for his players. The major leagues weren't knocking down his locker room doors, but he made sure that every single one his players used their baseball scholarships to graduate with a four-year degree. That was the focus of his program. At least it was until The Angel walked through his door.

Entry #102

"Johnny Angel"
- *Shelley Fabares*

I admit that my obsession with titling each journal entry with a song is stretched on this occasion (yeah, like I haven't done that before!). I wasn't Johnny anymore, and he wasn't my angel. Nevertheless, I just really think I'm so clever using the Shelley Fabares' song as a reference. Blame the Music Doctor if you don't like it!

In reality, Angel was not any kind of angel. The day I met him he had a mean and defiant personality that seemed driven by a deep and abiding hatred of someone or something. As Cal and I watched him glide through the outfield making extraordinary plays on fly balls, I understood why the local newspapers from the area dubbed him with "The Angel" moniker. He flew through the outfield as if he had wings. Whether it was catching a fly ball with his back to the plate like Willie Mays in the 1954 World Series, or it was leaving his feet to extend himself beyond an outfield wall, he was everywhere. As if reading my mind, Cal turned to me and said, "And you should see him hit."

With that, a line drive dropped about thirty feet in front of The Angel, and he rushed in to retrieve it on three bounces. He nonchalantly bent his glove hand only to have it trickle past him and come to rest many yards behind him on the warning track.

I remember giving Cal a pained expression. When he looked at me, I couldn't help but inject my vast knowledge in the area. OK, not really, but I did have something to contribute. Back in the day, most of us in exceptional high school programs learned the fundamentals of the game. Most of us didn't have the speed, size, or natural athletic ability to make it to the pros, but we never made a mental mistake when we played. Cal knew this, but The Angel considered himself too good to bother taking advice from anyone. This isn't to say that Cal hadn't made some strides with the 21-year-old phenom, but the player still resisted most authority figures.

Cal read my mind, and we discussed how he should have

made that play. He also told me of the other weaknesses that brought down the kid's game. He couldn't deal with the sun on fly balls, and he'd never learned to bunt. Though I never in my wildest dreams had the talent that this Angel (I dropped the "The" very quickly) had, I could still knock the shit out of him with my understanding of the fundamentals.

"Unfortunately, we are a low-budget program. After giving out scholarships, the school doesn't have enough money to give me an assistant. I don't have the time to do much one-on-one with him." I then made a decision that would irrevocably alter the course of my life. I offered Cal my services as a volunteer. *Do something good?* He'd done so much for me as a sponsor; it was time to give back. When I made the offer, I thought that Cal would be thrilled, or at least grateful. Instead, he just laughed. I was insulted. *Not good enough for you to use,* I thought. Just as quickly as the laugh began, it ended as he saw my disappointment (or was it anger?).

He explained. Every player on his team was trouble. He had sought them out in the ghettos and neighborhoods where no one else would go. Many members of his young team had been in trouble with the law and others would have been, had he not taken them away from the environment in which they had grown up. They came to play *for him*. He was a black man who offered them hope and a way out that no one else had ever presented. They respected him. However, some were still hanging on to their prior attitudes and lifestyles despite Cal's best efforts. My friend knew they weren't going to take to me very quickly. This is especially true for Angel. As Cal called him from the outfield to meet me, he told me to prepare myself. I will never forget Angel's first words to me.

"What the fuck do you want, jackass?" Cal turned to me in front of his rude player and said, "I should have told you that it's nothing personal. Mr. Angel here hates all white people." He was about to reprimand his player when I surprised them both and spoke up for myself.

"That's Coach Jackass to you." By my response, Cal assumed I had taken him up on his coaching offer. Oh, that's right, he hadn't offered me anything; I had offered him. A small, almost imperceptible smile flashed across his face. No such response came from Angel.

"This is a joke, right?" he asked, as he looked over at Cal whose only response was a meek shrug. He hoped that somehow I had a solution to our standoff, and I did. I took out a roll of money out of my pocket and flashed it at the obnoxious future star. Of course, he had no way of knowing that the twenty-dollar bill on top only covered a handful of singles with maybe one five thrown in for good measure. I knew this to be a fact because I never had more than thirty, forty bucks to my name. I acted with a bravado that came from "what-the-hell-do-I-have-to-lose?" ($28 to be exact, I would calculate later).

"My vast fortune is yours if you beat me in a test of baseball skill." OK, it wasn't just Angel who fell on the floor laughing, but the entire team now. They had gathered around us during our exchange. I was too busy acting dignified to glimpse at Cal, but I think he was laughing too. Angel broke up the hilarity with a simple question.

"And what do you get if you win?" More laughter.

"You agree not to be a prick to anyone who tries to help you . . . at least for a week." We stood toe to toe, but not eye to eye. He was at least ten inches taller than me. There was no more laughter.

"You're on . . . jackass."

"At least you're not a phony. You want to be hated for who you really are." I threw back at him.

"You can keep talking, but I won't keep listening."

"If ignorance is bliss, you must be the happiest person alive."

"Would it kill you to use deordorant, because it will kill me if you don't?" He had me there. I really was ripe after my morning run. We were in the middle of what we used to call as kids, a "good old rank out session."

"Enough," yelled Cal, trying to instill calm back into his practice. But, I wasn't done.

"Life is short . . . and so is your list of accomplishments." I had gotten in the last word and though I knew he would try to come back at me, he momentarily flinched. I had hit home. He was a local star and there were rumors he would be a high round pick in the next major league draft. Yet, he was not quite there yet. Behind that giant ego, I think he knew that.

"OK, Angel enough! Hear what he has to say," said Cal with a tone of finality.

"I propose a contest of who can catch the most fly balls." My last few syllables were almost drowned out by the uproar of laughs. He looked at me incredulously as I placed four cones on the outfield grass to create a 30-foot by 30-foot square. I told him that he could hit or throw ten balls into that area and see how many I caught. I would then do the same to him. Do I really have to write down the multiple laugh references anymore? The game was on.

He stood at home plate and patiently self-hit the balls to the area included. Of course, many of them missed their mark, and I stood in the grass and glared at him. Finally, a few soft drives came my way, and I handled them pretty well for a person who hadn't put on a glove in two decades. Angel then got wise to the competition and tried desperately to hit blazing line drives into the box where I stood. Two of the attempts not only handcuffed me but also almost took off my head in the process. He had grown tired of the effort, and so he softly threw three more high ones. My weary old bones handled these with no problem. His theory was that I'd missed two and therefore left it open for him to easily top my production. If he misplayed a handful out of a hundred flies, it was considered a bad day for him.

He motioned for me to change places with him so that we could fulfill his part of the contest, but I surprised him by motioning for him to come out to me in the field. With a look of confusion, he joined me in the box I'd made in the outfield.

"I'm too old to hit, and I can't throw that far, so let's just do this in the box. Just to be clear, I'm going to throw you ten flies. If you miss three, I win." Again, a look of confusion mixed with the smugness radiated throughout his entire being.

"Bring it on, Wanna-be Coach Jackass."

"You ready?" I looked around for a few minutes and located myself very strategically only ten feet to the left of him. I wasn't averse to playing mind games with him. I placed three slightly scuffed baseballs at my feet and held one in my hand. The implication was that I only needed that many to prove a point. I didn't know if that was true, but it didn't hurt my cause to get him questioning what I had up my sleeve.

I hurled the first ball straight up in the air. He wouldn't even have to move his feet to make the catch. That is if he could see it. I had thrown the ball directly in the overhead rays of the noontime sun. I didn't even try to restrain my glee as he not only missed the first fly but also had to avoid being hit in the head as gravity took its toll. Before he could even react, I threw the second ball, and again, he was lucky to escape with his life (or at least pride) intact. He muttered something like, "You sneaky bastard," only to see me launch the third round high into the air. This one actually did skim the side of his face on its downward flight.

"I win . . . and that's Coach Sneaky Bastard to you . . . or would you prefer Coach Jackass?" I rubbed in my victory as much as possible. I then picked up the last ball that lay at my feet.

"Double or nothing if I can catch the same throw." An interesting concept considering he had nothing to offer me. He nodded as I handed him the Rawlings pro model ball. He threw it higher than I could ever hope to and directly in line with the bright sunlight. If nothing else, the kid was strong and accurate, and I'm sure he really did expect me to miss his throw. I honestly believed that he wanted it to land squarely on my head and to put an end to my miserable existence.

With the skills that had been ingrained in me by the long-hated Coach Callan of McCarthy High, I raised my gloved left-hand way above my head. After a minor adjustment, the leather fingers shielded my eyes from the most villainous rays of the sun. Even before my stunted high school career, my Little League and CYO coaches had drilled my team-mates and me on this method of dealing with the sun. This had been in the era before flip-down sunglasses had made modern players lazy. As soon as the ball came to rest in my glove, I immediately turned to face him and gave him the most condescending smile I could muster. I had won, and because I had, Angel's life was changed forever. And so was mine. Yeah, maybe he was now "Johnny's Angel."

Entry #103

"You've Got a Friend"
- James Taylor

Here I go again, including a ridiculous title for my journal entry. "You've Got a Friend." Yeah, right. I don't think that Angel will ever consider me a friend. I'm the wrong age and the wrong color. However, he had come to respect me for what I could do for him. In the few days since our contest, he accepted me as his private mentor. Maybe he is using me and still hates my guts. I guess I'll never know. However, if he is using me, I'm also using him. After all these years, I finally feel I am doing something worthwhile, something with a purpose. I'm giving of myself to someone else, instead of just surviving. Maybe if I give enough of myself, the guilt I've felt will finally go away. I don't know. I just don't know.

I've been working with the entire team, and most of them call me Coach J. But Angel had his own name for me. I don't know if it's his sense of humor, or his ultimate inability to show me any respect by calling me a coach. When the players asked my last name, Cal respected my AA anonymity and said, "Oh, just Jack will do fine." Angel picked up on Cal's phrasing and calls me "Just Jack." Being just as childish, I have decided to call "Van the Angel" by his less reverential first name of Van from now on.

Entry #104

"All Right Now"
-*Free*

I've enjoyed helping Cal's team. I have awoken each morning of this past week and taken the 20-mile drive to Sugarloaf School. They greet me with friendly banter, and all of them (except maybe Van) seem to like me and appreciate the help I'm giving them. Van appears to hate me a little bit less than four days ago. It helps that I taught him how to bunt better and how to field grounders in the outfield. Is he grateful? I don't know, and I don't care. I did the right thing, and I am proud of myself for the first time in a long time.

Tomorrow will be the last day of my brief stint as assistant coach to Cal. More than anything I will miss the players. In working with them, I've gotten back the feeling of being alive that has so long been missing. These kids have their whole lives ahead of them and are filled with an enthusiasm I have found contagious. I feel like I want to start living life with the same excitement that they do.

It will be sad to say goodbye to them. It's only been a week, but it seems like so much longer. Perhaps I will take the drive up to their campus sometime this season and visit. In my decision-making process is the question of Cal's anonymity. Knowing him, he would probably welcome me warmly if I even gave him the slightest inclination of my desire to come up north for a while. Cal has separated his two lives by a considerable distance, and I don't want to risk causing problems for him. I'll have to think about this one for a while. The shortness of this entry is a testament to how busy I am today. I'm tired, and it is a good tired. This will be one of the last times I write.

Yeah, I feel good now. No, I am feeling really good . . . and maybe even decent. I can hear the guitar playing on the radio. The group Free is singing, "I'm alright now, baby, I'm alright now!" Maybe that is the sound of my redemption?

Entry #105

"The End"
- *The Doors*

This is "The End." Nothing can be construed from my

use of The Doors' song about incest and perversion. I just thought that those simple two words should be the last ones that I would write in this literary masterpiece. This journal is at its conclusion. It has served its purpose.

About eight months ago, I set out on a journey to rid myself of all the demons that have haunted me since that night in June of 1967. I know I took a brief detour on the "Reaper Express," but I made it through the other side.

I realize now that I will never forget. I will never lose the thoughts and doubts about what I coulda, shoulda, woulda done differently to save the lives of my friends. Helping real live human beings has enabled me to dull the pain. Padre has helped too. He has helped me understand I can't change the past; I can only make the future worth living. Of course, I realize that despite his claims, sometimes you can relive the past. I have done that through this journal.

Looking back, I now realize many things contributed to the tragedy that befell Those Born Free, and many of those same events contributed to my survival. Was there a reason? I've talked long and hard with Padre about being called to a higher purpose. I want my life to mean something. I know this falls under the category of better late than never. I've already wasted two decades wallowing in self-pity. While the journal made me feel worse for a time, it eventually did cleanse my soul. And now I'm done.

My writing has caught up with my life, just as it was always meant to. Any more entries would be a waste of time. I don't need it. And so, on this beautiful, sunny morning, I am going to say goodbye to this little marble notebook that has served me so well. I always thought I would pass it on to someone. I never did decide who that would be.

Therefore, in the immortal words of The Doors, "This is the end, my friend."

16

The Other Side of Life:
"Against All Odds"
- Phil Collins

IN FEBRUARY 1990, JOHN CIPPITELLI was forty years old. The flecks of gray hair that peppered his slightly receding hairline were noticeable only because the vast majority of his hair remained the same jet-black color that it had been in his youth. The crow's-feet wrinkles that framed his eyes were more a result of two decades of exposure to the tropical sun of the Florida Keys than of the natural aging process on his naturally oily Italian skin. Considering these factors and the obscene way he had treated his body for more than twenty years, Johnny Cipp, now Jack Paradise, was doing well.

Padre offered him a one room-one bath apartment above the garage that housed the St. Mary, Star of the Seas' vehicles. In return, Jack provided the church with some routine maintenance help. He mowed the lawns regularly, did some needed painting, and occasionally did substitute janitorial labor on the Immaculate Mary Elementary School. In his little covey, he had all that he needed: a bed to sleep in, a table to eat at, and a dresser to hold his clothes and his few valuable possessions.

Johnny's attention was drawn to his ever-present journal. A small smile came across his face as he looked at all the locations he had filled in the white swirls with either blue or black ink over the months. The blue ink made psychedelic impressions on the cover, while the black scribbles seemed to blend with the pre-printed black areas to create a solid non-distinct section of nothingness. Much like his life, times of creation and activity followed by decades of nothingness.

The water stains on the cover and the smeared writing on the interior reminded him of that darker time not too long ago when he had taken the coward's way out. The journal was truly a road map of his life.

He would now put away the book into the recesses of the very used Ethan Allen piece of furniture, perhaps never to be taken out again. It had served its purpose. He had relived his past and dealt with it the best he could. He had moved on. His talks with Padre and his work with Cal's kids had led him to value what he had become. It wasn't great, but it was a starting point.

As he opened the drawer to lay the book in its final resting place, he looked to the area where he had written the title in the white box in the center of the cover, "Journal of Johnny Cipp." Interesting choice, he thought to himself. This title struck him as ironic. Though much of the journal had been *about* Johnny Cipp, it had actually been written *by* his alter ego, Jack Paradise. In reality, he had lived more than half his life as this fictitious person. Who was he now? Was he Johnny Cipp, Captain Jack Paradise, Jack Paradise? Alternatively, was he some newly created persona that had yet to emerge? Was he some new entity? He liked Just Jack of all the people he had been. He would have to work on this whole situation eventually.

However, one sad truth had come to him. Because most of

his writings had concerned Johnny Cipp, the act of putting the book away meant he was forever putting Johnny to rest. He tucked the book under his clean but worn Sloppy Joe's tee shirts in the bottom drawer. Never to be seen again . . . he thought.

March 9, 1990 – 5 a.m.

Rising early was not an enjoyable experience for Jack Paradise. However, today he had to be up before dawn in order to drive out to Sugarloaf School and complete his tenure as the special assistant to Coach Cal. Perhaps it was the anticipation of the workout or the sadness of it coming to an end, but Jack found himself unable to sleep well the previous night. At 5 a.m., he finally surrendered any chance of any legitimate shut-eye. He looked around his small but comfortable room for some distraction to pass his time. He noticed for the first time the juxtaposition of two of the items he had brought with him from his previous life.

He picked up the guitar that had been his constant companion since he fled the Heights. When he had made his rapid and unplanned retreat from New York, he had depended upon Gio's kit bag for survival. His friend's clothes and essentials had long since decayed faster than Johnny's situation. Considering the depths to which he had sunk, this was not an easy thing to do. But he had clung to Gio's guitar. It had become more than just his weapon of choice in his musical career. It remained his security blanket in times of emotional turmoil.

This instrument would be in his hands as long as he could hold and play it. In reality, this remained one of the few objects in the entire world that tied him to his past life. The journal was now safely tucked in a drawer, and the guitar was in his hands. He had decided to strum a few chords of a song as a sort of eulogy to the journal and symbolically, Johnny Cipp's existence itself. Johnny was dead—long live Jack. The guitar, the journal and one other object that tied Jack Paradise to Johnny Cipp.

Twenty years before, Johnny had met with Gio in the Garden of Eden and he had heard Gio die while he cowered in the undergrowth a mere few yards away. Those moments had never been far from his consciousness. However, he seldom thought of the minutes leading up to their final meeting. Something in the room now drew him into that memory.

Johnny had been throwing a ball at the wall that lay next to the Garden of Eden when he had spotted Gio. He had done this "wall workout" his entire life. As long as he could remember, he had taken his glove to the park and spent hours heaving the ball against the concrete in an attempt to increase his ball handling skill level. When he formally stopped playing the game, he still went through the same routine merely to relieve tension, and there had been a great deal of that since *the* night in June. He knew that his workouts all those nights had served a far more devious purpose. If he hung out in the park long enough, perhaps one of the guys would just happen to pass. As the weeks flew by, the odds had grown shorter. By that night, there was only one member of Those Born Free who could walk by the yard. There was only one alive.

Finally, one night in September, Gio had shown up. Mrs. Cippitelli had directed him there when Gio had called looking for Johnny. The events that followed would forever be ingrained in Johnny's memory. Gio had died. Johnny had run. In his haste to escape, he had taken with him only one unnecessary object that was his and his alone, the glove that had been on his hand when he had spotted his friend. Why he had taken it at all was a mystery to him. At first, he could not leave it behind to provide proof that he had witnessed (at least heard) the crime committed outside the Garden of Eden. He also reckoned that he had kept it with him only because he had stuffed it at the bottom of Gio's bag as he made his retreat. But why had he kept it for twenty years? Damned if he knew. Who could have predicted that on this very week, he would actually don his beloved baseball glove?

He now looked down at that very same glove. It still bore the markings of his youth. It had the oil stains that were a bit heavy in some locations because of his overzealous attempts to preserve the leather. It still had the discolored scratch where the thumb had caught on a sharp outcropping while he had made a leaping catch against a chain link fence at Mater Christi High School. However, the most lasting mark on the leather was the heat branding that he had seared into the rawhide with the name Johnny Cipp. Though for twenty years the glove itself had served no practical purpose, he could not bear to part with the only object that had belonged to him in his former life. For all that time, it remained as a piece of proof that Jack Paradise was Johnny Cipp. He wondered if this small remnant of his past would ever insinuate itself into the life he had chosen? He would soon find that the answer to that question was a resounding yes.

When dawn finally arrived, Johnny threw the glove in the back seat of his twenty-year-old Toyota Corolla. The mileage he had driven this week probably equaled more miles than he had logged in any given month of his ownership. With a bit of hesitation, Van had taken to listening to Johnny's advice on defensive techniques. Most amazingly, he had become almost obsessive about learning how to bunt from the "old man." At first, he did it because he did not have a choice. His coach kept repeating the phrase, "A deal is a deal." Eventually, however, Van got over his reluctance to learn the skills that Just Jack had to offer. If their relationship had ended that day, all would have been well in both the worlds of Jack Paradise and Van the Angel. However, that was not to be.

March 9, 1990 – 10:33 a.m.

One last lesson for Angel. One final moment was all that was supposed to pass between the middle-aged, recovering addict and the major-league-bound, college senior. They would then go their separate ways, never again to cross paths in this lifetime. Jack Paradise would resume his life of playing guitar in the Duval Street bars, tending to the grounds of St. Mary's, and working very hard on his twelve-step program. He was upbeat from his experience with all the young hopeful players that Cal had brought to this Lower Keys getaway.

Van would finish the baseball season for his college team. He would then proceed to the major league baseball draft and a life of fame and fortune. Though still an angry young man, his tolerance for others had grown a bit, and he had learned a small lesson in humility.

They had made no plans to see each other ever again; there had been no phony exchanging of telephone numbers. It would be hard to say that they had bonded anywhere above the most casual use of the word. Van had used Jack to improve his abilities and knowledge of the game. Jack had used Van to make himself feel useful. The therapy of being a coach had proven significantly more successful than his aborted attempts at a physical fitness regime.

"Rematch, Just Jack," yelled Van, though the tone of his voice conveyed so much less venom than at the beginning of the week. He was indeed displaying the more competitive aspects of his nature. "You—me, in the outfield." An affirmative nod was all that met his challenge.

"Ok, big shot," crept out of the older man's lips. Cal looked at both of them like they were crazy, but his friend turned to him and said loud enough for Van to hear, "I can't lose."

"You have more tricks up your sleeve, Just Jack?"

"No!"

"Then why can't you lose?"

"If I win, I win."

"Yeah . . ."

"And if you win, I'm the best god-damned teacher in the universe to have taught a punk like you to catch flies in the sun." They both laughed.

Johnny yelled to Van to pick up his well-worn leather glove and bring it out with him. As the young player did, he looked down at the ancient piece of leather in his hand. He was going to comment on its age. Perhaps, he would tie in the antiquity of the glove with a comment about the age of its owner. However, after looking at the glove, he merely asked, "Who is Johnny Cipp?"

17

The Other Side of Life:
"A Question of Balance"
- *The Moody Blues*

June 5, 1990 (three months later)

CALVIN FREMONT HAD BEEN THE star of his high school team. If an outsider had posed the question as to which team he was the star of, anyone in his hometown of Waldo, Florida, would have responded, "All of them!" Offered scholarships to Florida State, Georgia Tech, and several other universities, he had a choice of not only which school to attend, but also whether he wanted the baseball, basketball, or football programs to pay for his tuition.

In the end, he had turned them all down in order to go directly into the major league draft in 1972. Given almost $100,000 in bonus money, he signed a contract with the Atlanta Braves and seemed to be on the fast track into their rotation. He mowed down the Class A batters with a combination of a fastball that clocked well over 90 miles per hour and a curveball that left opponents flat-footed as the men in blue called third strikes.

Unfortunately, it all came crumbling down before he celebrated his twentieth birthday. He suffered irreparable damage to his right knee when he collided with a runner while covering first base. Without a second thought, he was cut loose by a franchise that moved on without him. Left with no athletic career and no education to fall back on, Calvin Fremont drifted into an unemployed state that ravaged many other young black men of that time. Wallowing in self-pity, he soon found solace with bottles of just about anything that contained alcohol. Rock bottom had occurred three years later when an all-night binge had led him directly to a berth in a local emergency room. A kindly nurse had taken pity on him and had continued to stand by him even as he revisited the same destructive habits that had landed him in her domain in the first place.

In the end, her persistence had paid off. In *her* battle with *his* demons, she had won over not only his body but also his heart. On the third anniversary of his sobriety, Hannah Labeau and Calvin Fremont had wed in a small ceremony held in her hometown. Hannah's faith in Cal had paid off as he went to college after the wedding. Armed with a degree in teaching and coaching, Cal's love and knowledge of the game returned. He worked his way from the arena of high school athletics all the way up to the position in which he found himself today, head coach of a small Division I college program that now boasted a major league prospect on its roster. Venturing into violent neighborhoods in order to seek out talent, Cal Fremont openly spoke to parents about his trip to hell and back and vowed to protect their children from the life he had endured. He had a love of the game that shone through to all who met him and this proved a valuable tool in enticing recruits.

By far the most important factor weighing in his favor was his promise to protect his players from the "green giants" as he called them. Whether it was in the form of scholarships or professional bonuses, these forces offered quick money to a player, but no guarantees. They would take in, chew up, and spit out players who showed the slightest weakness. Cal had spent time getting over the anger he had internalized over his treatment. He swore that he would never allow any of his players to suffer what he had experienced. If his program offered you a scholarship, Calvin personally guaranteed it for four years, come hell or high water. Neither injury nor diminished skills were grounds for revoking a player's free ride, though the latter seldom happened because of the coach's exceptional ability to judge both talent and character.

Through good and bad, Hannah had stayed by his side and now was her time. While Cal was enjoying one of the best seasons of his career, his wife was busy working on the final touches of her own little Fremont team. The due date for the new arrival was a mere week after the end of the season. By most standards, this was perfect timing and planning on behalf of both Hannah and Cal. The right timing at least from the Fremont family point of view.

In a draft that would include many future major league stars, teams looked at Van The Angel with the same eyes that would be evaluating Jim Thome, John Olerud, Frank Thomas, Mo Vaughn, and Jeff Bagwell. However, all these stars were coincidently first basemen. Secure in the notion that they would resign their own elite player at this position, one team looked far beyond these future stars toward an outfield prospect from Florida.

If the New York Mets had known that Keith Hernandez was going to sign a free agent deal with the Cleveland Indians, events might have occurred differently. If Calvin Fremont III had not picked the very same week as the Major League baseball draft to enter this world, events might have happened differently. If Jack had not decided to take an extended run on a particular morning, events might have played out to a different conclusion. However, all these things did happen.

If swirling desires of fate had not created this chaotic pattern of events, the man known as Just Jack to a college team might have spent the rest of his natural born existence without ever leaving the state of Florida. However, whether it is called irony, or fate, or Johnny's own favorite word "synchronicity," all of these events had come to fruition. Because of all of these factors, Jack Paradise would return to the place of Johnny Cipp's childhood.

———◆———

"You want me to what?"

"You heard me," said the calm Cal to the obviously agitated Jack. "I want you to go to New York." He had expected a bit of reluctance to this suggestion, but nothing of this magnitude. Cal had invited his friend up to the team's complex many times during the season only to hear a variety of excuses. Now desperate for his help, Cal had driven down to Jack's home to plead with him. However, what he was now asking of Jack was beyond possible.

"Sorry, I just can't," was his adamant response as perspiration seemed to drift from every pore of Jack's being.

"Just hear me out. That's all I ask. I wouldn't have driven all the way down here from Marathon if I had any other choice."

"No. Nothing you can say is going to change my mind."

"Shit, I'm going to talk anyway." But Jack had already started to pull away. Cal grabbed Jack and spoke, "It's for Van."

"You mean the kid who barely tolerated me and . . ." his

voice trailed off, but Cal finished his thought.

"Hates white people!"

"You said it, not me."

"Technically, he only hates white men."

"A category I still fit into."

"Yes, but I've never seen him take to any one of you guys like he has to you."

"You guys? Is that some kind of racial slur from Calvin Fremont . . . of all people?"

"You know what I mean," said the now remorseful coach.

"Yeah, we were like best buddies," responded Jack with the sarcasm oozing on every syllable.

"He needs someone to be there in the city. He needs some guidance. I'm tied up here. You know, my wife having a baby and such. I mean, how often does a kid from a little Podunk college like mine get drafted in the first round by the Mets? The New York fucking Mets!"

"Never. 'Till you came along. And that's why you should be there," said Jack with some of the perspiration and agitation subsiding.

"And you know that family is the only thing that would keep me away from that signing ceremony. Hannah is having her C-section the day before the announcement, and you know I have to be with her. The athletic director agreed to spring for some travel money to have the program and the school showcased to the nation."

"There's got to be someone else."

"There is no one else. Besides, you and Van have a relationship."

"Yeah, if your definition of a relationship is that he hates me less than other white men."

"You really have to know the kid. He's had bad experiences."

"Is this where you lay a guilt trip on me?"

Cal's whole demeanor began to sag with frustration, and his previous enthusiasm seemed to give way to an acceptance that perhaps his recruitment efforts were going nowhere. He could not know that nothing would convince the Johnny Cipp inside Jack Paradise to return to New York City. . . and more specifically the Borough of Queens, where the New York Mets played their games. Nothing that Cal could say to Jack could make that happen except . . .

"OK, I won't push you. I guess Van will have to depend on his mother. She's a great woman. Raised him all by herself. Gave up everything for him."

"And the guilt trip continues."

"She raised a good kid."

"Who hates white men?"

"And I have tried to talk to him about that. But the anger in him is all-consuming and destructive. That's why I thought you were so good for him."

"Cal, until you yelled at him, he was calling me 'Cracker Jack' for the first two days I knew him." They both laughed a bit at that. Thankfully, Just Jack had prevailed.

"His father was white," blurted out Cal as if he had decided he was down to the last card he had to play. "The fucker screwed his mother and then took off before she even entered her third month of pregnancy."

"And Van has held an entire race of men responsible for one asshole's actions? His mother must have really laid into the creep," commented Jack.

"This woman wouldn't bad mouth anyone, ever. She still loves the guy and insists that someday he will come back."

"Hope springs eternal."

"She even named Van after the bastard," said Cal. Jack began to realize that he had never known the real name of the player that everyone had called either Van or "The Angel."

"What is his name? Van what?"

"If he has his way, he's going to change it legally to Van Angel. Bit of a sore point between mother and son."

"So, Van what?"

"Van isn't even his legal name. It's short for Giovanni . . . Giovanni DeAngelis Jr."

18

The Journal of Johnny Cipp

Entry #106 – June 7, 1990

"Redemption Song"
-Bob Marley

OH SHIT! I WAS SO wrong about the ending of the journal. Stupid little self-absorbed prick that I am, I thought the whole thing was over. How could I not know? I now need to write in this journal so they can all understand what's *going* to happen. It's no longer about the past, but it has become about the future. When Cal told me who Van was, everything fell into place. All the pieces that didn't quite fit twenty-three years ago now make sense. I need to tell Riet and Van all that I know. I must get this journal to them.

I'm finding it hard to write. I haven't slept since Cal's revelation. I never let on to him what I was thinking. I told him I still couldn't take the job, at least not officially. After he left last night, I decided that I *would* go to New York. But I would do it secretly and on my terms. I developed a strategy.

The first part of the plan would involve writing some final sections into this journal in order to complete the tale and reveal everything that I *now* know. I really don't want to rush, but I must.

Van left yesterday, and I'm going soon. I can't fly, and I can't even take a train. Despite the fact that those methods would be much faster, I can't use them. These more efficient means of travel require forms of identification that I just don't have. I can't take the chance that my Mickey Mouse quality ID will pass even the most cursory glance by a real professional. And so, I must drive to New York. I hope my ancient Toyota Corolla will weather more mileage in a day or two than it has in the last ten years combined.

I must go. There is too much at stake. Riet deserves closure. Van deserves to know that his father was a righteous man who would never desert his mother in her time of need. Perhaps, the contents of this book will vanquish some of the intense anger that has so permeated the life of that young man. More than that, I hope it saves their damn lives. They must be aware of the all-consuming hate found in the heart of Guy Provenzano. Though I don't even know if the madman still lives, I must warn Riet and Gio that Mad Guy will not have forgotten. He certainly won't have forgiven me or Gio or anyone related to us. Perhaps that knowledge will allow them to stay alive long enough for me to arrive. What I'll do, I really can't say. I only know that I must be there for them. I will make this right.

These few entries will be the end of my story. It is Van and Riet's story now. It doesn't matter what happens to Johnny Cipp or Jack Paradise. I've had 23 years more on this Earth than I deserved. I fully understand that I have squandered most of those years. It is time to pay the debt that I owe.

My hands are shaking . . . I understand what happened back then. Now things make sense. Gio knew Riet was pregnant, and that was why he was still around to talk to me. He had to tell her that he was going and that he would be back. He would've probably shared with her the entire experience of that night in June and the ensuing months. The deaths. The fears. He hadn't told her any of it. He hadn't seen or spoken to her since his arrest at the Driftwood Club. At first, it would've been because of his determination to resolve his legal situation. And then once the killing had begun, he wouldn't have wanted to put her in danger.

No one in the entire neighborhood knew of their love. He would've wanted to keep it that way. But with Riet's condition, he would've had a plan for her to join him. But that never happened. She never knew why he had disappeared. Yet, she had still believed in him. Riet had continued to instill her faith in Gio into the young boy. Only Van hadn't bought into his mother's passion. He had turned away from her devotion to my friend and had instead developed an all-consuming hate for the man he never knew, but with whom he shared a name. . . Giovanni DeAngelis. His nickname wasn't just a takeoff on his skill. DeAngelis literally meant "of the Angels."

And stupid me, the expert on song lyrics and meanings. Why didn't I pick up on the cues that Gio had given me? Where was my Music Doctor then? That afternoon before the audition, Gio had been anxious and distracted. He kept playing the same song over and over on his guitar, the same guitar that has lain at my feet every night of the ensuing 23 years. "Talk, Talk" by The Music Machine. How come I didn't see or hear the implications? Was I so excited about the audition? Was I too wrapped up in listening to the intense beat that I missed Gio's message in the song?

The opening lines said it all. The song was about "having a complication, - an only child." Johnny, you stupid fucking asshole. He was trying to draw you into his situation. And that last night in the Garden of Eden . . . *I'll be back to explain everything before I leave.* Why? So somehow, I could give Riet the help that she would need? So I could aid in their eventual reunion? I'll never know. And worse than that, she'll never know unless I tell her. I now know that the journal must have a final resting place in the arms of a mother and her child. They must understand the timeline of our disaster. They will have to trudge through my narcissistic journey to find the real depths of Gio's love for them.

And so, I go to them as fast as this rickety old car can take me. I travel a path that I never thought I would. Back to the Heights. Is there still danger waiting for me? It has been two decades, and the world has changed. Did Mad Guy ever know about me? I looked for clues from 1500 miles away and could never read the signs.

As far as I know, Gio's parents might still be alive. However, the last time I checked was a decade ago. To my thinking, their survival was a product of Guy's cunning. Gio had left a note saying that he was running away. When his life ended, everyone still believed that. Seeking his extended revenge on Gio's family would have disrupted that storyline to the detriment of Guy's innocence (in case any of the non-bribed police noticed). But do they still live? These are Van's grandparents.

I can only assume that my parents were left untouched for one of two reasons. Either Mad Guy didn't know about me, or he had left them as bait to lure me back. By the time I started writing my journal they were both gone, though I didn't know it. I had still been in the depths of my destructive period. By the time I found out, the journal had lost two of the people who would have benefited most from reading it.

Entry #107 – June 7, 1990

"Turn, Turn, Turn"
– *The Byrds (or the Book of Ecclesiastes)*
"And a time for every purpose under heaven."

It is time to make things right. It is time to save the inno-
cent. The question remains, is it also time to punish the
wicked or merely try to avoid them? I'd been a coward and
a loser in the past. I now have to act so that those people that
I had left hanging will have a future.

Van's name is now plastered all over the sports pages of the
Daily News and the *New York Post*. Though the sports writers
simply love nicknames like "Van the Angel," the authentic
persona of Giovanni DeAngelis Jr. will appear in type an
inordinate amount of times. Knowing the New York press,
there will be a nauseating amount of poor-local-boy-suc-
ceeds stories and numerous blow-by-blow descriptions of
his childhood. Beyond any doubt, the *New York Post's* cov-
erage will frequently mention his biracial makeup and his
Queens childhood.

How long will it be before Guy Provenzano notices this
loose end? Does he still care? What can I do about it? I owe
it to Gio to run interference in case Guy has decided to follow the philosophy of the "sins of the father shall be visited
upon the son." He is just crazy enough to hold a grudge all
these years later.

Time cannot pass fast enough as I wait to make my journey to New York. Cal told me that the press conference was
to be Sunday evening. It's Thursday afternoon now, and I
am finishing the pages of this journal. A bit of car trouble
has held me up, but a friend should have it fixed by morning. I'll put this journal in overnight express and be on my
way. But what will I do when I get there? Should I knock

on Riet and Van's door and say *"Hey, now that you read my journal I guess you know that your father didn't desert you. He was murdered by a psychotic nut case who may or may not want to kill you too. But have a nice day and enjoy your moment of glory."*

And who was I to them? Was I Johnny Cipp or was I Jack Paradise? How do I explain my situation? *While your father was dying, I hid a few feet away shitting my pants in fear. Oh, and, by the way, 23 years later I'm still a coward and didn't tell your mother or you what happened.* I hadn't spent nearly enough time as Just Jack teaching Van to bunt and field to pull that off without getting my ass kicked.

When my car crosses the Throgs Neck Bridge, and I find myself again in Queens, will there be a time to reap and a time to sow? Will there be a time for every purpose under heaven? And what will I do with that time?

I knew that I had to resist going straight to Van and his mother and presenting myself to them with the journal in hand. I think the confusion about who I am (or was) might overshadow the implications of what is in the journal. Or, what if I mailed it to them and they merely tossed it away, thinking it written by someone who wished to capitalize on Van's coming fortune? As I finish my last few entries, a plan is beginning to form in my head. There *is* someone who can sort through my self-indulgent ramblings and cut to the core of what Riet and Van need to know. I have an answer. Riet and Van, I hope that you've gotten this far and understand all that I've done.

In moments, I will be placing this book into an envelope. I need only to get to the post office on Whitehead Street so that I can send this away by the fastest possible method. I think I have a plan. It may mean the end of Johnny Cipp and Jack Paradise, but I owe it to Gio. I only exist because Gio covered for me both that night at the club and the night that he met his end. I've wasted most of the years given to me, but no more. I have always wondered if there was a purpose to my life and now I know. Van and Riet must live even if it is at the ultimate cost to me. I see what I must do. This will be the last time that I write in this journal.

PART
4

"Lives in the Balance"
- Jackson Browne

19

The Other Side of Life:
"I'm Going Home"
– Ten Years After

June 8, 1990

A FRIDAY MORNING IN JUNE IS a hectic time for any teacher, especially one who teaches high school English. Though classes had ended the previous Wednesday, she had an incredible amount of end of the year writing projects and essay tests that she had to grade. Her days were filled with red ink and the necessary comments to explain those markings. Given the option of staying home and grading the papers or seeking the companionship of her colleagues, Maria had chosen to go to school.

William and Samantha had taken the bus to their elementary school, and Maria was putting the finishing touches on her makeup when the doorbell rang. Upon answering the door, she spied a uniformed driver standing in his blue summer shorts and matching top, and she didn't know what to make of it. She had never received an overnight express package in her life. Because of this, her first reaction was hesitation in ripping open the red, white, and blue box. She stood transfixed by the actual packaging. What could it all mean? Should she wait until after school to open this unexpected arrival?

In the end, it was the six-letter word *urgent* that helped her to make a decision. Not noticing the tab that allowed easy access to the contents, she instead lifted a pair of scissors that lay beside her as she walked into the kitchen with the box. Neatly cutting the box open, she pulled out most of the contents found inside. On the table lay a handwritten note with her name on top and a black marble notebook that she had inadvertently laid face down on the table. The first thought that came to her mind was that this was a last-ditch effort by a failing student to get into her good graces by proffering a notebook full of writing. Only whoever had addressed it, had written "Maria" rather than "Mrs. Carlson."

"What the hell. Why am I playing Sherlock Holmes?" she mumbled to herself and turned the book over. It was then that she saw the words, "Journal of Johnny Cipp." Was this real? How could it be? Who was even still around who knew of their love of so long ago? She gently placed the book down and lifted the note. How could she ever forget the unique script that had written so many letters of love during their brief but real time together?

Dear Maria,

I am so sorry for all the hurt that I have caused you. Yes, I am alive and well. I should say that finally, I am well. This journal will explain that statement and answer all the questions that I should have answered in 1967. I cannot express how I felt for you so long ago better than I have in this book. Those feelings have never died. I know that I have missed out on what would have been a wonderful life with you and that is entirely my fault. I know that you did find happiness with someone else and that you are doing well. Because of that, this will be the only contact that I will have with you. Staying away is the best course for me to take. You should know that I never did find someone else like you and that is my punishment for the horrible way I treated you.

Once you have read this journal, you will understand that you must pass it on to the person listed below. This is a matter of life and death. The journal explains. You will always be in my heart.
Johnny

She found a second note in the box and placed it aside in confusion. It was not addressed to her. She hoped that reading the journal would make clear who the recipient would be.

Before she even picked up the book to read, she walked over to the phone on the kitchen wall and dialed the number of her mother-in-law. She explained that an emergency at work would keep her busy all day and asked if Patricia Carlson could take the kids off the bus later in the day and bring them back to her house. Jason was working overtime and would not be home until late. This taken care of, she then called school and explained that she had a family emergency and that she would not be in that day. She would take care of all of her responsibilities by Monday.

With all these details taken care of, she sat down to read the journal at approximately 9:45 a.m. By 9:46, the tears had started to fall and would not stop falling until 1:16 p.m. when she concluded the final page. The sadness and happiness invoked by Johnny's tale soon gave way to a sense of urgency when she realized what was at stake. She must go right now. She knew that at some point she would have to explain the whole situation to her husband. However, she decided to hide the evidence until that discussion was at a time and place of her choosing. The note and book were coming with her to Cambria Heights, but she had to dispose of the box.

She lifted it and headed toward the back door to deposit it in the outside garbage can. It was then that she realized that the box was not empty. Turning the box upside down on her table, she watched as one final object encased in crumpled paper rolled out onto the table. She opened the wrapping, and its contents fell to the flat surface, creating the soft pinging sound of metal on Formica. Her hand went to her mouth as she stared at the silver band that lay there and she read the words written on the scrap torn from the notebook.

I am in a good place in my life. I am where I am going. My journey is over.

"Strangers When We Meet" – Part 3
- The Smithereens

June 8, 1990 – Afternoon

She pushed the automatic locks down on her car doors. She had taught her children not to be afraid of people based on their race. However, returning to the Heights brought back all those memories of the overwhelming fear that had been ingrained in her in the 1960s. Now she found herself not only physically back in the place she had feared, but also mentally back in the days when racism had dominated so many people's thoughts and actions.

She was doing something that she would never have done in the old days. She was crossing the line. It didn't make a difference today. The area was now completely African-American with a high percentage of West Indians living in the homes that had been the memories of her youth. In reality, the neighborhood looked good, but old fears died hard. She turned onto Springfield Boulevard, and her heart skipped a beat. How many times had she and Johnny walked this path on the way to Carvel for shakes and cones? How many times had she laughed at him as the "big superstar" was struggling to get all his equipment over to Jimmy Mac's basement on the red Radio Flyer wagon that he had found in a junkyard?

Focus, she reminded herself. Do what you need to do and get the hell out of here. She had a name, address, and a task to fulfill. She looked at the weary and worn black composition book that lay on the seat beside her. Why couldn't she have seen this 23 years ago? Her life might not have been different, but the knowledge in this book would have made it easier. She tenderly stroked the cover. She tried to hold back the tears, but all at once, they fell in torrents down her cheeks. "Johnny, I would've understood."

The turn came up for Colfax Street, a place she would never have ventured in 1967, but in 1990 she would do so for Johnny. She looked again at the address and the name then turned onto Francis Lewis Boulevard. She knew she was getting close to her destination. She knew now from reading the worn testament in the seat beside her that Johnny had walked this very street one fateful night years ago and that was part of the reason why she was here now. What he had seen and what had happened had been the reason for all this.

She was at the location given to her. She shut the engine and briefly gave thought to the safety of her late model car and again accused herself of racism. She clutched the worn book in her hand as she walked the cracked but clean concrete sidewalk toward the house. She spoke softly to herself, "Am I freakin' nuts?" The bell seemed to stick, and for a brief moment, she half wished that no one would answer the door. She lifted the book to her chest, shook her head with a sigh and again exclaimed under her breath, "Johnny, Johnny, Johnny."

Suddenly the door opened, and a tall, athletic black man faced her. His muscles bulged from a tightly fitted t-shirt that read, *New York Mets,* and his demeanor betrayed contempt for this middle-aged white woman who seemed so out of place in the Heights. If his mother had not just given him the lecture about being a polite human being to strangers, he might have said, "What the hell do you want?" Keeping his mother's wishes in mind, he simply said, "Yeah?"

"I need to . . ." she started to say before a pretty but tired-looking woman nudged the younger man aside. Quickly losing interest, he walked back into the interior of the house.

"May I help you?" The words seemed an effort. Maria assessed that this woman had not had an easy life. Premature strands of gray could be found intertwined with her longish straight hair. Though she had obviously once been a beauty, the years had taken their toll. Maria immediately knew that this was the person she had come to see. Scanning her eyes back and forth between the older beaten woman and her arrogant young son, she knew why she was here. She could put together the pieces of the puzzle. She could see all the mistakes of long ago. Maria knew what had happened to this woman. Riet had been hurt like so many others. Part of her newfound wisdom came from her ability to perceive the obvious, but most of it was from the book that she held in her hand. That book that had helped her to understand so much would now do the same for another.

And so it was that Maria Romano Carlson finally came to meet Harriet Tubman Carver—Riet. Maria remembered an entry from the journal. In another life and time, they

might have sat and watched while Gio and Johnny barbe-
qued some burgers. Together they would have hustled their
offspring away from the still flaming charcoal that had been
used to prepare the kind of feast that the two families would
have often shared. In another time and place, their husbands
would have taken out their guitars and serenaded these two
women jointly. Perhaps, "Wonderful Tonight" by Clapton.
What might have been?

Instead, Maria looked directly into the eyes of Riet and
said, "You'll want to. . . no. . . you need to read this. It is
about many things and some of them you must know. I hope
it helps you the way it did me." With those words, Maria
relinquished possession of the worn and tear-stained black
and white marble composition notebook. She knew that this
was the right thing to do, but it was still hard to give up her
last link to Johnny. Maria also handed Riet another note
that had been included in the package.

Riet,
This book was always meant for you. I just didn't know it. Now
your lives depend on you reading and understanding its contents.
~ Johnny Cipp

Riet recognized the name immediately and tried hard to
place it. *Oh God,* she thought. I know who this is. He was
the friend who . . . a flood of memories washed over her
brain.

"There are answers in here . . . and if you need me to fill in
any the blanks I'll leave my phone number and you can . . ."
Before Maria could finish her sentence, the woman took her
hand and said, "Come in. Please, come in." As they entered
the clean but ancient kitchen, she motioned for Maria to sit.

"I've waited a long time for answers, and my guess is, so

did you. So why don't we just go through this together? The young man eyed the white interloper with suspicion and concluded that his mother had gone insane. He was caught completely by surprise when the stranger faced him and said, "You'll need to read this too." The young man took the book from the table and held it in his hands with a look of confusion.

"What the fuck?" he began only to be admonished by his mother to watch his language. He then continued, "I didn't read anything this long in my four years of college."

"Maybe you should have," quickly responded his mother.

"You both need to read all of this. It might not all mean something to you, but you will see the parts that do," Maria interrupted. Anger flared from the young man.

"I have places to go. I'm not wasting my time on this shit." He raised himself to leave, which brought on the first traces of emotion in his mother. On the verge of confrontation with her for one of the few times in his life, he lifted the book in disgust and motioned to throw it on the floor. In doing so, his eyes caught sight of the cover for the first time.

"I . . . I know this name," he whispered in astonishment. A look of confusion replaced the fury that had been in his eyes. *The baseball glove . . . Johnny Cipp? Just Jack?* With emotions swirling in his head, he looked again at the cover and read aloud, "Journal of Johnny Cipp." He then sat with his mother and Maria. The cracked cardboard cover had become soft with its years of use and so it made no sound as they opened it to read.

Hours later, Riet and Van finished the journal. Despite the fact that they now realized that their lives might be in imminent danger, a look of calm overcame both of them. Riet had answers. Van seemed almost drained of all the venom that had consumed him every waking moment of his life. Though some anger and hatred still dwelt in his heart,

Van was at peace more than he had ever been in his short and volatile existence. At first, his emotions centered on the father he had never known. He did not know what to feel toward this Johnny Cipp/Jack Paradise character who had let down the person he now understood to be his father. Van set aside those feelings because of his growing desire to find and destroy this Guy Provenzano, wherever the snake called home. As if reading her son's mind, Riet gently touched his hand but said nothing. Maria broke the silence.

"I don't know where we all go from here, but I'll be with you if you want."

"I think that my son and I have to take this all in before we know where to go from here."

"My husband is a cop. Do you want me to call him to report the threat to your son's life?"

"My son is going to be out there for the whole world to see for the next few days. He is going to be on newspaper pages and the sports' spots on the local news. Do you really think that it is possible to hide this from anyone?"

"I'm sorry. I was just trying to help."

"I know, but Sunday night is going to be the biggest day of Van's life. He is going to be introduced to the New York media and be proclaimed the savior of the New York Mets."

"But before I save the Mets, I am going to kill that fucker," let loose Van who had held back his feelings while his mother was speaking.

"You're not such a big shot that I can't wash your mouth out if you continue to use that language in this house. And you're going to do no such thing," interrupted Riet.

"Ma, he killed my father."

"A father that you hated a few hours ago, despite me telling you to have faith."

"OK, you were right."

"Then listen to me now. We're going to be vigilant at all

times. You are going to that press conference. He took away our past; I won't allow him to take away your future. You're going to have all the glory you deserve."

"And money. Don't forget money," added Van with the first minor smile to grace his lips since Maria had knocked on their door.

"I don't want any of this to hurt your moment in the sun. Perhaps afterward, we will think how to protect ourselves. This lunatic would not think of doing anything to us while you are in the public eye."

Seeing their minds made up, Maria got up to leave. She had wanted to stay longer because this entire day had brought her back to that time. But her real life waited. She needed to see her loving husband and adored children. She needed to return to *her* life. She too had "gotten where she was going." She reached into her purse and started to write on a piece of paper that she had withdrawn from the clutter of makeup, wallet, and other sundry items that made the leather enclosure weigh double digits.

"This is my phone number. If you need help with anything or just to talk about things, give me a call." Maria faced them. The moment was awkward with each not wanting their time together to end, but knowing that it must. Riet rose from her chair, took a few steps, and then tightly hugged the surprised Maria.

"We will see each other again," said Maria. With a simple nod to Van, she walked out the door and into her car. She left the Heights.

"Homeward Bound"
-Simon and Garfunkel

June 8, 1990 – 6 a.m.

Jack Paradise left Key West by early morning on Friday, June 8, 1990. As the sun was rising, he drove northward on the Overseas Highway. Would this be the final time that he viewed the white coral, tropical vegetation, and never-ending horizon that he had come to love in the last few years? He was heading home, perhaps never to return. Was he still Jack Paradise? Or did returning home reinstate him to his former status of Johnny Cipp? Only time would tell if he would endure long enough to be called anything at all.

As he passed Bahia Honda, he marveled at the former railroad bridge that had once been the only real link between the Lower Keys and the outside world. In one devastating moment in time, a hurricane had humbled humanity into submission by submerging large sections of the Florida Keys. The bridge had never been used after that storm. The hubris of mankind to think that nature could be harnessed and controlled for its own purposes. Was his quest to save Van and Riet from the wrath of Mad Guy any less futile?

As he crossed out of Key Largo at mile marker 108, he started to feel the gravity of his mission. Soon he would be in what he thought of as the *real* Florida. The Keys were some magical way of driving to a Caribbean Island by car. Florida, north of Homestead, was just Florida. Now his thoughts turned more solemn. He hoped that Maria had received his package and made her way to Riet and Van. They had to know what was coming.

By now Maria had his journal. He had so many reasons not to send it directly to Van and Riet. However, if he were honest with himself, he would have realized that this was all merely a justification for his actual motives. Riet and Van *needed* to read the journal. He *wanted* Maria to read it.

20

The Other Side of Life: "My Little Town"
- Simon and Garfunkel

June 9, 1990 – Sunrise

IT WAS STILL EARLY WHEN he arrived in the Heights. He assumed that none of the people he wished to save had yet to awaken. He had decided to shadow Van and Riet for the next few days. If he saw anything dangerous, he would intervene. What he would do then was up for grabs. He had no weapon, and his fighting skills were significantly rusty. He thought that he might call the authorities, but that was an absolute last resort. That call could save Van and Riet's lives. However, the police could not be trusted 23 years ago because the Provenzanos had paid many of them off. He could not risk that this was still the case.

Finding himself with no immediate task, he decided to ride the streets of his childhood. He turned left on Colfax Street and headed down Murdoch Avenue toward Springfield Boulevard. He could not help remembering that night when he had inadvertently stumbled upon Riet and Gio. It had been the only time in his life that he had talked to this person who had figured so prominently in his best friend's life. He could not believe that this same person now figured so prominently in *his* life. It was to his eternal shame that he had never gotten to know her better (add it to the list). So long ago, her broad smile and relaxed manner had impressed him. Her quick wit and sense of humor had put him at ease. Her stunning looks had been unforgettable. Now she and her son were the last links to Gio and the past. He had to do right by the two of them—for Gio's sake.

As he crossed the line, he saw that it was no longer the stark divide it once had been. What lay before Johnny were neat rows of well-maintained houses with minuscule lawns that were neatly manicured. Johnny used to joke that mowing grass in this area could be done by scissors. Apparently, the local stores were selling their share of this utensil.

If the whites had stayed, could this have been the model of integration that New York City had so desperately needed? No one would ever know. In fact, Johnny wondered how many of the residents of this area even knew or cared about the struggles and violence that had torn these streets apart two decades earlier? So much had changed in the area, and in the world.

He rode his car up what had once been the cobblestone hill that lay perpendicular to Springfield Boulevard. The stones no longer remained. They had been lost to a modernization project that had blacktopped every little quirk in the city highway system into the same bland looking cookie-cutter roads. This was the final stretch of pavement before he arrived at *his* house. His parents were long gone from this area and this world. He had never seen them after that day and never had a chance to tell them he was sorry. Johnny was racking up the guilt points on his hometown tour.

As he looked at the exterior of his former home, there

were happy memories. He started his visual trip down memory lane in the basement. Though most practices took place at Jimmy's, occasionally they changed to his house. He still remembered little Lisa Donohue and her friends peering into the open windows and fawning over the group like they were stars out of a teen magazine. Yes, it was fleeting fame, but fame nonetheless.

His eyes next rested on the main floor of the house. How many nights did his family spend in front of the color television that was the one great luxury his parents could afford after all the bills? How many times had he and his father marveled at the trick endings of *Twilight Zone* or laughed at *I Love Lucy* or *Red Skelton*? And all the family holiday celebrations that had taken place in those cramped but loving quarters. He wondered what had ever happened to his aunts, uncles, and cousins. Did they even remember him?

His eyes finally landed on the highest point of the narrow home, the attic. This converted storage space sweltered in the summer and froze in the winter. The long and winding steps made access to his room a physical activity rather than merely providing an entryway to his private chambers. Still, when he had climbed those dozen steps, he had entered his kingdom. It had been the place where he had read his comic books and made the models of his favorite movie monsters. It had been the place where he had refought the battles he had seen in the films and had played his music and composed songs. It had been the place where he rested and relaxed. It was where all his thoughts and dreams had taken flight. It had also been the place where Maria and he had found their very few moments of privacy.

He hadn't known he was leaving it for the final time. He had never said farewell to his sacred refuge. Like many things in his life, there had been no closure. How long had his parents left it in its final state? When did his mother remove the dirty clothes from the floor where he had left them? When were the comics removed from the shelves? When did the poster of Brigitte Bardot on a motorcycle finally get removed from the slanted wall that arched over his bed? What happened to the remnants of his musical career? Did some other young boy try to make music with the acoustic guitar that he had worked so hard to master? These thoughts haunted him as he returned to his car and continued the tour of his childhood town.

On his way through the Heights, his next stop was at the boarded-up site of the former McAvoy candy store. Mrs. McAvoy could not make a go of it without her husband and son. Perhaps even with them, the business would have failed. The Cambria Theater, site of many of the monster movie double features of Johnny's youth, was also long gone. In its place stood a Pentecostal church. Not much call for penny candies before entering that place. Where had Mrs. Mac and her three daughters gone?

He continued his trip down memory lane to the site of Bracko's house. Its charred remains had long since been replaced by a house that had *not* been designed to match every other home on the block. While houses throughout the Heights were not identical to each other, they were usually the same as the rest of the houses on *their* block. The one glaring exception would always be this monstrosity of architectural design that lay as an anomaly located mid-block of 219th Street. Perhaps, that was how it was meant to be, a living memorial to those who had died there. No one would ever know except for one lone visitor from Key West.

This was all too much for Johnny, but he knew he must go on. He needed to see the reality that went along with the stories he had written in his journal, and that had led him to his final stop, only one block away. He started singing the words softly to a Cat Stevens' song, "Don't You Remember the Days at the Old Schoolyard?" The Music Doctor knew that he needed to go to the Garden of Eden. Some of his first happy memories had been of chasing the *spaldeens* hit into the bushes during his regular stickball games. *Don't you remember the days at the old schoolyard? We used to laugh a lot.*

He could not and would not visit Gio's home. This would be where he would remember his best friend. Here he would remember how Gio saved his life while Johnny listened to him take his last breaths. He owed it to his friend to go there. As he grew nearer, other thoughts wandered through his mind. This had been the place where Tony Provenzano had gone from schoolyard bully to mindless child in a few moments of idiocy. He had witnessed the tragedy that had cost Tony most of his brain functions. Johnny had been a part of the rescue team that had saved his life. Perhaps that had been a mistake. Though Tony had become a friend to the group, Johnny always felt that Guy's anger and viciousness had escalated because of his brother's tragedy.

Then there was Bracko. He had first met the guitarist here. The memories of his lonely and abused friend ran through his rambling thoughts. The master guitarist had been found sitting in the weeds playing to the smiling but glazed over face of Tony. Yes, so many memories were in this place that he now approached.

Only the Garden of Eden existed no more. A Board of Education decision had crowded more and more students into the insufficiently sized building known as P.S. 147. The solution to this problem had been to construct annex buildings throughout what had once been the playground and its garden. Gone was the place that represented so much of the story of Johnny's life. Students sat and learned their reading, writing, and arithmetic directly where he had played stickball and softball. Children sat gazing at their teachers above the sacred soil that had once been the Garden of Eden. A small smile formed on Johnny's face as he thought of the irony. *Yes, Music Doctor, you've sent me another Cat Stevens' song.* He softly sang to himself. *But tell me, where do the children play?*

He did not dwell on the thought for long. Perhaps this was a message from somewhere above. *Yesterday's gone*; get on with what needs to be done.

June 9, 1990 – 6:45 p.m.

Johnny allowed himself the luxury of dinner. He thought long and hard about where to eat. Eventually, he chose the Sherwood Diner over the border in Nassau County. This had been where his mother had toiled all those years ago to help pay for his education. No one who worked in this classically styled restaurant would remember her, with many of the servers appearing to have not even been born 23 years ago. He needed to go there anyway.

After his experience with the lost Garden of Eden, he wanted to see and touch something that had not changed. The booths and freestanding tables appeared to be the same ones that had graced the Kentile floor that remained after all these years. Whoever owned the establishment now saw no reason to upgrade the facilities in light of the lower standard of customer who now frequented the location. Gone were the snobbish matrons who had looked down their noses at the hard-working waitress from the Queens side of the border. Gone was the wafting cigarette smoke that had inundated the place while the rich spent hours discussing how well they were doing in their lives. If their situation were to be judged by the minimal tips that were left to the hard-working staff, they obviously were not doing as well as they boasted. Johnny enjoyed the ultimate misfortune of this place that had probably contributed to his mother's early demise. He contemplated the fact that his actions had also been responsible for her failing health. He finished his sausage and eggs and exited the diner more depressed than ever. Time to focus. In memory of his mother, he added a 30% tip to the cost of the meal and left. He drove back to Riet's house to continue his surveillance.

He knew the exact house where Gio and Riet had had their many hidden meetings. He only hoped that Maria had gotten the journal and its message to Riet in time. As he stared at this home, he wondered how it was that she still lived in her family's original location. What was her story? No, there was no time for a snowbird investigator to look into this one. If he had not heard Van's throwaway comment about his mother living in the same house for 30 years, he wouldn't even have known that this was the same place. Nevertheless, here he was skulking a half a block away in his beat up old car with Florida plates. Would this attract the attention of neighbors, or worse, the police? He hoped that both groups were just too busy with important matters to notice a misplaced white face in the neighborhood.

"In My Life"
- The Beatles

Harriet Tubman Carver had given birth to Giovanni DeAngelis, Jr. on a cold winter night. At her side were her mother, Gladys Carver and her uncle, Thaddeus Carver. Both were furious with the name given to the young boy, but Riet was adamant in her choice. She insisted that someday Gio was going to return. Despite the conditions of his birth, both mother and uncle adored the little boy, and they filled his early years with enormous amounts of love and attention. Unfortunately, Uncle Thad had some bad habits that led to some bad actions that put him away for life without parole.

Gladys Carter worked two jobs to keep her daughter and grandson both in their house and eating regularly. Riet never knew if it was the strain of this punishing work that was a factor in her death at age 44 from diabetes-related symptoms. At 24, Riet found herself with a child and no visible means of support. While pondering her fate after the death of her mother, she took care of her responsibilities with a sadness and efficiency that surprised even the self-confident young woman. She dreaded the ordeal of emptying her mother's locker at her daytime lunchroom job. She knew her mother had made many friends during her years there. She now had to face those friends and their abundant sympathy and sadness. After a good cry with a group of women who really cared about her mother, she received a message to report to the principal's office. The thought caused the first smile in many a day to cross her face. *I'm being sent to the principal's office.* Once there, she was introduced to the energetic leader of the school, Principal Charlotte Davis.

Boss Charley, as all the workers and quite a few of the students called her, was a strict but fair black woman in her mid-forties. Her blemish free coffee skin was accented by a semi-long "Afro" hairstyle that betrayed her passionate role as a civil rights advocate throughout the turbulent 1960s. Now, however, she had become content to fight her battles for justice and equality one student at a time.

Charley welcomed Riet into the room with a huge hug that caught the younger woman by surprise. Because Van had been a student at the school for a few months, Riet only knew the woman as a person of authority in her son's life. Little did she know that her stern exterior masked a heart of gold. Riet would learn all this in the ensuing years, as the two became close friends. It all started that day when Charlotte Davis offered Riet Carver her mother's job.

By 1990, Riet had worked for 17 years at P.S. 147. At that time, it had become clear that she would not be doing so for much longer. Based on the articles in all the local papers, Van would receive a contract that would guarantee his mother would never work another day in her life. Though she would miss seeing her younger friend, Charlotte Davis rejoiced in the knowledge that the world had finally repaid Riet for all the shit it had thrown at her for so long.

Riet had told her son she wanted none of his newfound wealth, but he would hear nothing of it. Though anger and hate had dominated his view of the world, he had nothing but undying devotion for the mother who sacrificed her own happiness for the sake of his success. Both mother and son agreed they needed advice on how to proceed best with their financial future. Her good friend Charley had the answer. Her nephew had worked his way through college and law school and was now a top-notch lawyer. He would represent the young athlete in all of his negotiations. As a favor to his beloved aunt, he would do it all free of charge. Someday, if Van were happy with what he had done for him, he would be paid back. More importantly, Riet and Van trusted Earl Ruffin to do right by them.

It was Earl who knocked on Riet's door at precisely 10:30 a.m. on Saturday morning as Johnny Cipp began to watch the drama unfold.

21

The Other Side of Life:
"Money for Nothing"
– *Dire Straits*

June 9, 1990

TOM MESSINA DID NOT READ a great deal. He had quit school midway through 10th grade to go to work for the Provenzano family. At first, it was just a bit of selling junk here and there. However, by the age of 23, he had graduated to a heavy dose of enforcement. He did not care for books, magazines, or for that matter, even newspapers if what he read was not about sports.

He was a fan of the Yankees and Giants and followed the horses when they were running at Belmont. However, even with his limited reading matter, he made an effort to know about all sporting events, even those that held no personal interest for him. In this way, he might cull specific information that would help his boss adjust the betting line for his lucrative bookmaking operation. If he picked up some info on a quarterback injury or a pitcher with a sore arm, Guy would give him a smile that made him feel he was earning his keep. Find out that a star player had been doing a tad too much partying before his next game, and Tom might even get a few bucks thrown his way. No, Tom Messina did not read too many genres of writing, but he did obsess over the sports pages of the *Daily News*, the *Post*, *Newsday*, and even occasionally, the *New York Times*.

While in the midst of one of his forays into sports investigation, he came upon the news of the Mets' first round draft pick being a local kid. He would be returning home for a press conference at Shea Stadium this Sunday. Perhaps, there was a way to parlay this situation into some money. Maybe the kid would throw a big game or something like that. Overthinking gave him a headache. He decided that he should just give his boss the info and let him decide what to do with it. That was why Guy was the boss, and he was just some lowlife who read the papers. It sounded like a plan to Tom Messina.

"You're fucking kidding me? After all these years. So, that little faggot was holding out on me," said Guy Provenzano speaking to no one in particular as he sat in his office with Tom. In reality, not many people would understand his anger upon seeing the name of Giovanni DeAngelis in print. It had been so long ago, and those who had witnessed his reign of terror in 1967 were no longer around.

Sammy Crespo had taken a bullet in the face in 1970. Sal Timpone was serving multiple life terms in Sing-Sing for getting caught doing a hit for Guy. There was no chance that he would turn on his boss. In return for his loyalty, Guy supported the Timpone family in a comfortable lifestyle. Besides, snitching on a Provenzano would decrease the life expectancy of the informant to an amount of time measurable on a stopwatch.

Of all the followers who were aware of the madman's vendetta against Those Born Free, only Richie Shea remained on the scene. Long since retired from the police department, Shea finally started to use the law degree that he had earned at night school. Guy found it amusing that his cousin collected a government pension and a mob salary at the same time. Moreover, both incomes were on the books.

Having seen *The Godfather* movies, Guy envisioned Shea much like the role of consigliere Tom Hagen as played by Robert Duvall. He would be the WASP face that the organization needed as a front on occasions. The emergence of Giovanni DeAngelis *Junior* was one such occasion. Now Richard Shea, lawyer and corporate hotshot, would be sent on a mission.

"This could mean more money for your client than he is going to make playing ball. The endorsements are guaranteed for at least three years," spouted the exuberant Richie Shea.

"But we will need more information about the type of business that Van will be endorsing before I allow him to sign an agreement," replied the still wary Earl Ruffin.

"This kid is not just another client to me. I'm going to protect him like family."

"I would expect nothing less," quickly responded Shea. The now middle-aged ex-cop had come a long way since his days as a detective. His red hair had toned down a few shades and widow's peak had begun to form on his hairline. Flecks of gray had intruded into his sideburns. His Brooks Brothers suit fit perfectly on his six-foot frame, and he exuded the appearance of professionalism that was necessary to convince clients of his abilities.

"We're not rushing into anything," continued Earl Ruffin, who himself stood every bit of the same six-foot height of his opponent. It served him well in the eye-to-eye stare down that now ensued. Though not as wealthy as Shea, Ruffin wore decent clothing bought at Macy's on sale. It fit well and served its purpose. Earl Ruffin was not usually trying to impress his clients in the same manner as Shea. Though only in his early forties, Earl Ruffin had had a harder road to follow to reach his point of success. His fit body was a remnant of the athleticism of his youth. However, he was not good enough to have colleges come calling with scholarships. He had therefore taken the route of the City University of New York and attended Hunter College. Though tuition was free to city residents, his daily living expenses and commuting costs put some strain on the family finances of his two loving parents who insisted that he concentrate on his studies rather than work part-time. The real expense came when he was accepted into Fordham Law School. There he had encumbered a multitude of loans he would probably be repaying until he started collecting social security. The financial help of his Aunt Charley had reduced this debt. He could never repay her; she would not accept it when he offered.

"Just be a good lawyer and a good person. That is all the repayment I need," had responded Aunt Charley. The only request that Charlotte Davis had ever made was that Earl Ruffin take care of the legal and financial matters of Giovanni DeAngelis, Jr. Damned if he was not going to do right by this kid and his saintly mother. As Van's legal representative, Shea had contacted Ruffin with a proposition for the young rising star. Pro-Services, Inc. was interested in paying extravagant money for the endorsement of its products and businesses. Earl Ruffin assumed that the company's name was related to the fact that they provided services to professionals of some sort, or that they were a quality organization. He could not know that the "Pro" in Pro-Services was short for Provenzano.

"OK, here is the straight story," began Shea. "The owner of Pro-Services is a very private man. He does not want any publicity for himself, and he will not tolerate any bad publicity for his company. Therefore, he wants to meet your client personally before the deal is done. He does not want anyone to know about this until the deal is completely sealed."

"So, what are you proposing?"

"First, let me talk money."

"I'm listening."

"Pro-Services is offering a sort of blank check to Van. Whatever amount the Mets offer him per year, we will give him the exact amount per year to endorse our company. Furthermore, we guarantee our deal for three years."

"What's the catch?" Earl Ruffin always felt that if something sounded too good to be true, the odds were that it was precisely that—too good to be true.

"The only catch is that Van has to meet with the owner first hand to receive his approval."

"And who is the owner?"

"Again, he wants no publicity. What's to stop you from announcing the meeting to get some press for your kid?"

"I wouldn't do that," replied Ruffin, now a bit miffed that his integrity had been called into question. "What exactly do you want from us?"

"The meeting will be Sunday night right after Van's press conference at Shea Stadium."

"I know a good restaurant in Astoria where we can bring the parties together," offered the now intrigued Ruffin.

"No, I don't think that you get it yet. My boss is a very private man. No public places."

"Then where?"

"His yacht is docked at the marina adjacent to Shea Stadium. After the big excitement at the ballpark, Van will meet my boss in the privacy of the very comfortable confines of his boat."

"This is very unusual."

"My boss is very unusual. But don't tell him I said so," replied Richie Shea in an attempt to add a bit of levity to the occasion. "Besides this is the only way the deal gets done. It's my way or the highway."

Earl Ruffin had a 10:30 meeting on Saturday morning to discuss this proposition with Van and Riet.

Richie Shea had informed Guy Provenzano about every detail of his meeting with Earl Ruffin.

"Do you think that he suspects anything?" asked Provenzano.

"How could he? He doesn't even know that there is anyone after his precious client.

"His unfortunate client and his mother will never be seen again. Just another black youth cut down in his prime."

"What about the lawyer?"

"Collateral damage."

Johnny Cipp watched Earl Ruffin leave the Carver household around noon. He still could not figure out if this was one of the bad guys or not. Johnny had a gut feeling that this man was on Riet and Van's side, but this was too serious a situation to make assumptions based on no available facts. He decided to leave his post and follow the stranger.

It was tough to be inconspicuous with his beat up old car and its Florida plates accented by his white face behind the wheel. He knew that his surveillance would have to be short-lived. Finally, after a quick stop at a fast food restaurant, the stranger pulled up to a storefront office on Linden Boulevard, not far from where Jimmy Mac's family candy store had been. Johnny watched as he put the key in the glass door that read, "Earl Ruffin, Esq., Attorney-at-Law." It made sense that Van would hire an agent, especially since his coach could not be there to advise him. No problems so far.

Johnny returned to the Carver home by mid-afternoon to continue his full-time vigil. He didn't have to wait long before he saw Van exit the house. He wondered if Riet and Van understood the potential danger of their situation. Had they even seen the journal? Had his strategy of keeping his distance from them been the correct choice? He even contemplated calling Maria to find out if she had accomplished her mission. That would be a sticky situation. In the end, he decided to take a wait-and-see attitude.

Within a block, Van came upon a group of men around his age shooting hoops at a basket and backboard hung haphazardly from a telephone pole. It struck Johnny as ironic. Two decades ago the chaos that had ensued in his neighborhood had been precipitated by the installation of state of the art basketball courts in his childhood playground. Now those hoops had given way to portable classrooms and the destruction of the play area for children of all races. The games in Cambria Heights had returned to the streets. Full circle.

As Van approached the group, the smiles were broad, and the handshakes followed an elaborate ritual reminiscent of some secret organization. In reality, these greetings represented a lifetime of friendship and camaraderie. Van had come home. To these friends, he was not the superhero who would be signing a major league baseball contract soon. He also was not the son of a white man. Nor was he a person being stalked by a psychotic killer. He was just Van, another black kid looking for some hoops on a Saturday afternoon.

Was it Johnny's imagination, or was Van wearing the most gigantic smile he had ever seen on the young man's face? Perhaps, it was seeing his friends again. Maybe it was seeing his mom and tasting her home cooking. Possibly, it was the prospect of the money he would soon have coming in that fed his smile. Or maybe, it was the fact that some of the deep down pain and anger that had so infused his soul had been erased. His father *had* loved his mother and had not deserted her.

Johnny watched Van play with a gusto that he had never seen before, even when the natural athlete had patrolled centerfield in Florida. The Mets would probably be angry that their prospect now risked injury in a pickup game of basketball. However, they probably were not any more upset than his mother who held *the journal* in her hand as she wailed warnings that Van just ignored. Van did not seem to understand that there was a monster out there.

Van played until there was no longer enough light to even shoot the basketball. With hours of sweat clinging to his t-shirt and skin, he made his way home after bidding his friends farewell. He would sleep well tonight. This would not be true for Johnny Cipp who had resigned himself to a very uncomfortable night in the back of his car. The dirty front seat was all too visible to passing traffic on the street. The back seat, though more cramped, and even filthier due to the deposit of debris, was slightly more private. Florida law allowed for the deep tinting of windows as a protection against the UV rays of the tropical sun. This feature of Johnny's Toyota let him sit unnoticed while fulfilling his role as guardian angel. However, that in and of itself was a dilemma to said guardian angel. What exactly was he doing?

He was following Van practically twenty-four hours a day, but to what end? He could have just sent a warning in the form of the journal and let matters go at that. That could have been enough. However, Johnny owed Gio more effort than that. Johnny owed his life, and he had determined that if necessary, he would give that life to save Riet and Van. And so, he watched and waited with little concept of what he would actually do when the shit hit the fan.

Perhaps, Guy Provenzano was unaware of Van's existence. This was highly unlikely due to Mad Guy's obsession. But where was Guy, and what was he doing now? Where was Johnny's snowbird detective now that he needed him? Being gone so long, Johnny had no conception of what path Mad Guy's life had taken. Maybe he was dead. *No such fucking luck* thought Johnny to himself. No plan at all. Just watch and wait, and sleep in the back of his smelly car.

Around 9:30 a.m., he observed life in the home. Soon, Riet and Van exited the house and drove away in her old 1985 Dodge Omni. Johnny followed at a safe distance while the mother and son worked their way down Springfield Boulevard and made a left onto Linden Boulevard. He probably should have deducted where they were headed by the quality of their dress and day of the week. About a quarter of a mile up the boulevard, the car came to a stop and parked in front of the former location of the Cambria Theater, which was now a Pentecostal Revival Hall. He smiled. He was glad to see the Carvers were taking time to give thanks for the fortunate turn their lives had taken.

Johnny had once been extremely religious. Where had it gone? Where had his whole life gone? He was just about to turn 41 years old. Was it too late to salvage a fulfilling life once this drama had played out? Then again, would he still be alive when this whole affair was done?

As they entered the hall, Johnny looked for a location to wait out the service. He knew that these types of services could run for many hours. He knew he had to hunker down for the duration and he looked around for an appropriate spot. He noticed that directly across the street from the church stood the local branch of the public library. In his day, the building would never have been opened for business on a Sunday morning. However, in the ensuing years, the government had repealed the blue laws, and to many people, Sunday had merely become Saturday, part two. Seeing the lights on and people roaming its aisles of books, Johnny saw an opportunity.

As he entered the front door, the memories flooded back to him. Though there had been minor changes to the setup of the facility, the layout remained virtually the same as in his younger days. While many things had changed in the Heights, it was evident that money for improvements in this educational venue had not been a priority. The dark oak shelves remained situated in roughly the same locations as when he had found *The Autobiography of Babe Ruth* for a third-grade book report. Even now, Johnny was sure he had at least one book that was 23 years overdue.

He roamed the same aisles, hoping that no one would challenge his right to do so. He even found the same shelf where he had years ago vandalized the woodwork. The "JC and MR" scar still marked the location where he and Maria had stolen a brief kiss. Years of sanding and re-staining had been no match for the work accomplished by his pocket knife a lifetime ago. He had to focus. He had to worry about the task at hand.

Ten magazines and almost three hours later, Van and Riet emerged from the worship hall. Johnny followed them home and watched a progression of well-wishers visit the mother and son. Johnny grew hungry smelling the odors of the home cooking that wafted from the kitchen window and seemed to permeate the entire city block. The visitation of the star would soon end. It was almost time for Van to leave for Shea Stadium and his crowning moment.

June 10, 1990 - Evening

In 1990, Todd Van Poppel had received a signing bonus of $1.2 million from the Oakland A's. He had been the top pick overall of baseball's draft and therefore used that leverage to become an instant millionaire. Giovanni DeAngelis, Jr. was the New York Mets' first pick in that same Major League Baseball draft and stood to join the ranks of wealthy sports figures. Though not the level of Van Poppel's contract, Van the Angel had agreed upon a substantial $500,000 deal. With the impending matching agreement with Pro-Services, Inc., the young player also stood to reach the lofty status of millionaire. All he had to do was complete the press conference and then meet the owner of some mysterious company on his boat.

The Mets had been more extravagant than necessary in their offer to the young future star. They desperately needed to regain the trust of a frustrated fan base that had seen them fail on and off the field since their miracle win over the Boston Red Sox in the 1986 World Series. The ensuing seasons were judged failures in light of the hope engendered by that one moment of glory. Management had needed to show the fans some positive moves and therefore had chosen to make the most out of the publicity surrounding the signing event.

Van entered the stadium sitting on the back of a Cadillac convertible at the conclusion of a game that saw the home team shut out by the Philadelphia Phillies. It seemed only fitting that the offensive hitting star of the future be unveiled on a night when the Mets had failed to score a single run. He emerged from the gates closest to the famed apple in left field. This icon was raised whenever a home team player hit the ball over the fence. Sadly, the apple had laid dormant for much of this recent home stand.

As the player and management entourage circled the field on the way to home plate, Johnny listened from outside the stadium. He could have bought a ticket and waited inside, but his feeling was that even someone as crazy as Mad Guy would not attempt murder in front of thousands of witnesses. Better to be ready to follow when Van, Riet, and their lawyer left the stadium through the player exit. If Provenzano was going to make a move, this was the one location that he would be sure to find his target. Johnny did not know if the madman had the resources to locate Van before this moment, or had even tried. However, here and now, Van was out in public and had become an open target. Johnny needed to stay as close as possible.

The crowd cheered as Van held up his new jersey with its Mets' logo on the front and the number 23 emblazoned on the back. He had chosen the digits because it represented the age he would be on his next birthday. He also hinted that this would stand as the age at which he would play in his first major league game. This was a bit presumptive because this would allow very little minor league training before making the Show. The Met fans were not privy to all these machinations and cheered mainly because the number choice stood as a direct challenge to their cross-town rivals. The New York Yankees perennial fan favorite and star, Don Mattingly, wore the number 23. Let the games begin.

After the obligatory speech making and cheers, the ceremony was over. The Mets officials offered to take their new player out to dinner, but his lawyer respectfully declined the offer with a feeble excuse about Riet being ill and Van wanting to take her for some fresh air. And so, Riet, Van, and Earl exited Shea Stadium and headed toward the docks at the Flushing Bay Marina. All three envisioned the matching $500,000 endorsement fee being offered as an opportunity beyond belief.

While the lawyer remained in the dark concerning any threat to his clients, Riet and Van had discussed the journal and the possibility of danger in their actions. From what they had read in the journal, this Provenzano character was a low-life gangster who would be slinking around in dark corners in a cheap suit and slicked down hair. There could be no danger in dining with a billionaire on his yacht. Johnny followed Van, Riet, and Ruffin as they went to meet their fate.

Richie Shea met the prospective victims not far from the exit. On the false premise of granting them privacy, he had arranged to meet them only after they were out of the limelight. In truth, he wanted to meet them outside of any light, lime or otherwise. There would be no witnesses to their departure aside from Earl Ruffin. However, if everything went according to plan, Richie Shea would keep him distracted for the evening.

Johnny followed at a safe distance. He could not be sure who this new player on the scene could be. He kept his distance. There was no way of him knowing that this was one of the few people in the entire universe who might be able to identify him as Johnny Cipp. Having been given a photograph of the band by the DeAngelis family, he had carried the likeness of Johnny with him until the day he retired from the police force. Now years removed from that position, he still remembered the face of the fugitive that his cousin had so long sought to destroy.

The broad expanses of concrete that surrounded the Mets' home field spread out in all directions and served their purposes as both walkways and parking lots for the venue that at times could boast attendance of over 50,000 people. On its north, south, and east boundaries, the paved areas reached their termination points at public highways, train stations, and shops that either had predated the stadium or had grown up around it. Only the westerly direction defied this urban sprawl, yielding its pavement to the dark boundaries of Flushing Bay and ultimately the East River. No commercial buildings existed on this side of the stadium except those built to house the recreational craft docked at the marina.

Johnny surmised that this must be the small group's ultimate destination and stealthily made an end run around them when the sidewalk found its way under the Whitestone Expressway. The immense concrete pillars that allowed this thoroughfare to rise above the streets leading to the bay offered cover to the covert actions of Johnny. Moving quickly and quietly, he arrived ahead of the group as they made their way to the entrance gates of the marina. However, the chain link gate was locked, admission only permissible to those with a passkey. He hid behind a Lincoln Continental left close to the entrance. The owner's selfish conclusion that he was above walking from the parking lot to the gate worked to the advantage of the hidden spy. He had yet to pick up anything from their conversations that would tell him if this was going to be a dangerous situation for Riet and Van. The fact that the expensively dressed stranger had waited to meet them in relative darkness gave Johnny a bad feeling, but he needed more information before he could act. Then as if on cue . . .

"Go straight down the central pier until you can't go any further, and then take the left extension pier to the last slip," said Richie Shea.

"You're not coming with us?" asked a surprised Earl Ruffin.

"No, in fact, neither are you."

"What does that mean?"

"Relax. This is a good thing. You and I are done with our part of the business. My boss is a man of his word. Van signed for $500,000, and he will get a contract from us for that exact amount on Monday morning. There is no more negotiating necessary. All that is left is for the boss to meet personally with Riet and Van and like them."

"And who is this mysterious boss?" replied the now agitated Earl Ruffin. "And who is he to judge them?"

"He's the one who is laying out half a million dollars on an untested athlete to promote his company. Hey, listen, if you want to walk away now, I'll call a cab to take you all home. No harm, no foul."

"No, wait. We'll go," said Van almost panicking that Ruffin was going to blow his opportunity to set up his mother for life. He had already decided that he would take the Mets' money and he would give his mother all of the Pro-Services cash.

"Are you sure?" spoke Riet for the first time since they had left the press conference. She looked around and noticed the seclusion and darkness of their situation. "You know the book that we got Friday."

"What book?" asked both Shea and Ruffin? Riet realized that she was not ready for either of them to know the story and quickly covered. "Oh, a book of helpful hints for living long and prospering." Van laughed. His mother often quoted *Star Trek* and had just now diffused the situation by citing the Vulcan salute given by Spock.

"Yeah right, I think it was even called, *Live Long and Prosper*," offered Van who was both changing the subject and telling his mother he got the inside joke.

"OK, let's do this," said Riet, her confidence and pride in her son showing.

"I'll take Earl home," quickly offered Shea and then turned to the other lawyer and added, "Is it OK if I call you Earl?" Ruffin nodded his assent but did not feel comfortable with this whole situation. Shea threw his arm around Ruffin as if they had been the best of friends for many years. In reality, it was his job to find out what made the black lawyer tick. When Riet and Van never returned from their midnight cruise, the paid-off dock workers would say that the two had been left off and taken a cab to destinations unknown. Earl Ruffin would indeed be the only person who even knew where they had gone after the press conference. Richie Shea would get to know the real Earl Ruffin in the next few hours and then report to his cousin Guy. The boss would then decide the next course of action. Would they threaten him? Would they bribe him? Or would they simply put a bullet in his head?

"C'mon Earl, let's get to know each other." The two lawyers walked away. Behind the Lincoln, Johnny Cipp hung his head in frustration and whispered in a voice only he could hear, "No, Riet, dammit. Don't go."

As Riet and Van started down the long concrete dock, Johnny realized that he had a problem. Not wanting to follow too closely, he had to stay hidden until the mother and son had walked some distance from the entranceway. This allowed the gate to swing shut and lock, cutting Johnny off from his task. He now had to hope that some other boat owners would be leaving soon so that he could have access to the docks. He watched hopelessly as Riet and Van turned off the concrete path onto the adjoining wooden pier to the left. Soon it might be too late.

He then noticed a couple exiting a large cabin cruiser docked at one of the nearby slips. A sixtyish bald man with a large belly and shit-eating grin held a stunning blonde-haired woman under his arm. She might be of legal age, but Johnny doubted it. This was obviously a match based on something other than undying love. As they approached the entrance, they saw Johnny's face pressed through the six-foot-high wrought iron rails that made up the outer protection of the marina.

"Could you let me in, please? I left my key card on my boat," begged Johnny.

"Suurrrre," replied a voice that slurred way too much for someone who was about to get behind the wheel of a car. Johnny watched as the drunk old man made three swipes at the key card pad before the young blonde had to relieve him of the card and use it correctly.

"I hope you're driving," offered Johnny to the girl.

"I . . . I don't have a license," replied the young girl confirming Johnny's suspicion about her age. She obviously had not had as much to drink as her companion, and probably not enough to mask the torture of having spent time with this scumbag. Johnny's only thought was that she must be desperate for money to have been with this slug.

As the gate opened, Johnny did not even wait for them to exit before he slid passed them and started running as fast as he could to catch up with Riet and Van. He still was not 100% sure that they were in danger. Then he saw them walking up a metal gangplank onto a large, but not overwhelmingly sized boat. This was not the water retreat home of a wealthy businessman unless he wished to turn off any prospective clients who were of Italian descent. This was someone who was saying to the world, "Fuck you," . . . literally. The name of the boat told Johnny that beyond the shadow of a doubt, it belonged to Mad Guy Provenzano.

Italian-Americans going back to their arrival on the shores of the New World had always spoken with certain bastardized phrases of their native tongue. Foremost of these was the Italian version of the "F" word. In reality, the phrase that Italian mothers chastised their children not to repeat was actually the "V" word—Vaffanculo—translation, "fuck you." Later generations distorted this to "ba-fangul" or just "fangul."

As Johnny looked at the writing on the stern of the small yacht, he realized that Guy Provenzano had taken this phenomenon a step further and created a phonetic synonym to announce his attitude to the world, probably without the world getting it! *Fuck you*, he was saying to everyone and everything in his screwed-up universe. The glaring headline on his boat told the whole story at so many levels . . . *Fun Ghoul.* Not only was he telling the world where to go, but also in English, he was describing himself to a tee. *Ghoul (n) – a fiend who shows morbid interest in things considered shocking or repulsive.* Moreover, all of the mayhem that he created was "fun" according to the Provenzano code of conduct.

Yes, the name worked on so many levels, and it was the final clue that confirmed to Johnny that this was where their showdown would take place. *No, fuck you, Mad Guy,* was the only thought on Johnny's mind as he closed in on the boat's location.

———————

"Welcome aboard," said a voice from the distant reaches of the vessel's flybridge. The stout middle-aged figure made his way down the ladder onto the lower deck. As he crossed the ten-foot distance to where Van and Riet waited, he proffered his right hand, "So glad to finally meet you both." Riet's fears were somewhat allayed by the pleasant attitude and broad smile presented by the owner of Pro-Services.

"Glad to meet you too," was all she had to offer.

"Sorry to have to make you wait a little longer, but I have to go up top and steer this baby out into open water."

"Oh, we would be happy to stay right here. No need to waste time and gas taking us away from the dock," suggested Riet.

"Nonsense, I won't hear of it. Gas and time, I have. Besides the view of the New York skyline is stunning out in the East River." Already loosened from its mooring, the boat had started to drift and needed to be controlled. Now only a foot from the dock, it soon would be in danger of floating into another craft if he did not start the engines immediately.

"But . . ." muttered Riet. It was all she could muster as she watched the overweight figure climb the ladder from the lower cockpit area back up to the flybridge. He eventually reached the platform that extended approximately seven feet high over the lower level. Her eyes followed him as he took a seat in one of the two pedestal chairs that served as a comfortable perch from which he could guide the craft. Riet noticed that there was another figure seated next to their host. That person had yet to move or speak.

"He never told us his name," offered Van interrupting his mother's thoughts and adding to her growing suspicions.

"I'm sorry," yelled the figure at the steering wheel as he briefly turned around, "I forgot to offer you the champagne that is in the ice chest to your left. Have some and make yourselves comfortable in the lounge chairs while I get us out onto the river. No more than ten minutes, I promise."

"But who are you?" yelled Van. The Cummins engine engaged and the deafening noise effectively ended any chance at a conversation between the bridge and the two sitting almost 15-feet away in the back of the boat. It seemed as if there would be no further contact between them for a while, and Riet and Van settled into the comfortable seating. They pondered whether they had made a mistake.

The massive engines began to gain strength and had just started to propel the *Fun Ghoul* forward toward open seas when a leaping man hurtled through the air and landed on the swim platform of the departing boat. The *Fun Ghoul* by now had pulled almost six feet away from its berth, and the man could not maintain his footing on the moving vessel. Never having the distance to make it over the transom to the main deck, the body crashed into the rear fiberglass wall that separated the swimming platform from the rest of the boat. Turning to see who had alighted on the surface behind them, Riet and Van looked up to the tower to see if their host had noticed the commotion. He had not. They peeked over their lounge chairs and the transom wall to gaze at the still figure that lay prone on the flat swim deck. They stared at the motionless body for a few seconds wondering if the impact of the collision with the rear wall had done damage to the apparently unconscious man who lay face down. It was only the non-slip nature of the surface material that kept him from rolling off into the bay.

Riet and Van looked at each other, both sets of eyes questioning what they should do about this turn of events. It was then that they saw signs of life from the body. Slowly but surely the head lifted, and an arm reached out for help. Van grabbed it and pulled the stranger towards himself. Still, the body started to roll toward the water. Riet now also grabbed the elusive figure to prevent it from going overboard. Both mother and son found themselves unable to move for fear that the man would be lost to the sea. Time flew by as they tried to solve their dilemma and somehow send a message to their host that there was a critical situation at the rear of his boat. It was then that the man regained consciousness. Van was surprised when he quickly found himself face to face with the stowaway.

"Hi," spoke the bloody mouth that stared at him.

"Just Jack . . . this is Just Jack, Ma," yelled the excited Van. However, as he turned to his mother, he noticed that her hand had flown to her mouth to suppress a scream. There were tears in her eyes when she spoke softly.

"Johnny?"

22

The Other Side of Life: "Showdown"
– *The Doobie Brothers*

WHILE JOHNNY WAS TRYING TO re-establish conscious thought, the *Fun Ghoul* had worked its way past LaGuardia Airport, its Sunday night flights providing additional noise that covered the action at the rear end of the boat. Soon, Guy Provenzano cruised past Rikers Island and stared at it with contempt. This infamous prison would never see him in residence. This he swore.

Oblivious to his new passenger, Provenzano was intent on making his way to the seclusion provided by the Long Island Sound. In a short time, he would pass under the Whitestone Bridge, and not long after that the Throgs Neck Bridge. He would then be in open water. Provenzano might have his passengers wondering at the length of the trip, but he didn't care. Maybe the champagne had taken the edge off, and they were unaware of their predicament. A smile grew on his face.

He looked over at his brother Tony who sat still on an adjacent chair peering out into the ocean. He had not moved since they had arrived at the marina and he had latched on to the cushioned chair on the flybridge, maybe his favorite seat in the whole world. Tony remained silent. He had not spoken at all in over two decades. His mother had taken him to every conceivable doctor in the metropolitan area with absolutely no results. The younger Provenzano brother had gained so much weight that climbing the ladder to the flybridge was becoming a challenging test of his physical ability. However, riding on his brother's boat was the one activity in life that seemed to give him any joy. Whenever Guy took him on the *Fun Ghoul*, he sat in the same position as he did now. He found great pleasure in staring out at the sky and sea. He particularly enjoyed the wind blowing through his hair, which he had regrown to a wavy dark reminder of what a stunningly handsome lady-killer he had been in his youth. Now Guy likened his brother's favorite pastime to a dog sticking its head out of a moving car. This always elicited laughs from the minions who surrounded the madman.

However, tonight he would take care of business alone. On the rare instance when he took care of the dirty stuff himself, he wanted no witnesses who could turn state's evidence against him. That was how you stayed out of Rikers. Only Tony would be here for the show. This would not have been his choice, but he always took him on the boat when his mother was visiting his father in the nut house. Guy had convinced her that she could only handle one mental defect at a time. Either her husband or her son had to go. *See you around, Pops.* For his part, he wanted nothing to do with *the retard* (as he referred to his brother most of the time). Still, he knew that he had to pick his battles intelligently. Mom Provenzano still held some of the purse strings of his father's wealth, and it was best to pretend to have a good heart, at least until his mom kicked off. If this meant taking his brother on an occasional sea cruise, so be it. He was just a lump. Wherever you led Tony, he followed quietly behind. It was no big deal for him to come along tonight. If there was one person that you need not worry about testifying against you, it was a retarded mute. Therefore, confident in his mission, Mad Guy guided his vessel under the Throgs Neck Bridge and into the waters of the Long Island Sound. Yes, he would put an end to this chapter of the story in unforgiving waters of the Sound.

———◆———

"Who the fuck are you?" Any pretense of civility had left Guy. He now had them where he wanted them, and he discarded the persona of a business executive. This was the way he had always planned it. However, he had never planned on a third person being on board when he exacted his final revenge. "I repeat, who the fuck are you . . . and what are you doing on my boat?"

"Hi, I'm Jack Paradise, and I represent the college that Van attended. Just came along for some moral support and advice."

"Third time's a charm. Who the fuck are you? And once again, how did you get on my boat?"

"Oh, the two nice gentlemen at the dock helped me on just as you were getting ready to leave. I didn't want to disturb you while you were driving, uh steering, whatever, you call it on a boat." Johnny knew very well what it was called. As Jack Paradise, he had spent an inordinate amount of time on the fishing boats of Key West. But the less that Provenzano knew about him, the better. Mad Guy apparently did not recognize him.

"Those two will never be mistaken for gentlemen, and they would never have let you on the *Fun Ghoul* without my permission. So, I repeat . . ." started Provenzano again, but this time he was interrupted.

"Who the fuck are you and what are you doing on my boat?" mimicked Johnny. He had no plan and was just playing for time by keeping the conversation going as long as possible while searching for something. However, it soon occurred to him that perhaps mocking an insane killer who had been hunting for him for over twenty years was not an ideal stall tactic. His last barb had pushed Mad Guy over the edge.

"I don't care who the fuck you are . . . and it really doesn't matter how you got on this boat because you're never getting off it." With that, he withdrew a large KSC Glock 19 with 155 mm silencer and pointed it at them. They had arrived in the center of the body of water that separated Connecticut from Long Island only minutes before the verbal exchange had begun. Provenzano had shut off the engines and pressed the button to lower the anchor before turning to his guests. He had expected to charm them for a bit longer before they suffered their ultimate fate, but the sight of this stranger had caused him to reconsider his course of action. He feared that two adult men could somehow overcome both him and his little friend, Mr. Glock. He therefore never proceeded down the ladder to the deck that held his prey, but instead spoke while standing at the edge of the raised flybridge.

"Riet . . . Van, I'd like to introduce you to Mr. Provenzano, or Mad Guy as his friends call him . . . just never to his face."

"Oh shit," mumbled Van, and Riet dropped her head in disgust for the stupidity of her judgment in falling for this ploy.

"Sorry, the 'Mad Guy' label still fits I assume." He knew he was pushing it, but the grudge that Provenzano held toward Those Born Free was dwarfed by the hatred that had been building inside of Johnny for most of his adult life. He didn't care what this asshole thought. With that, a shot from the silenced gun flew inches over his head. With the sound of the waves lapping on the side of the boat, the suppressed discharge of the weapon was virtually inaudible. Johnny only realized that Mad Guy had fired at him as the bullet passed the top of his head.

"I didn't miss. That was a warning. One more word out of your mouth and the next one will be between those two eyes of yours." The rocking motion of the boat caused Provenzano temporarily to lose his balance. He decided that it would be more secure to sit down. The flybridge floor extended over the rear deck and provided shelter to the cockpit area nearest to the entrance to the galley. He lowered himself so that his rear end found a resting place on this overhang while his feet dangled freely off its edge. This was a bit risky, but he still was 8 to 10 feet away from the three prospective victims, and his dangling feet were at least 5 feet raised above the lower deck. He was far enough away to discourage any plan of attack that the three of them might hatch. And he had the Glock!

"Now to you two," started the madman again, only to see Johnny flinch as if to move toward him. He carefully aimed the gun at his head and said, "Right between the eyes, if you move, that's what I promised you. Remember?" Johnny stopped short.

"Not moving," answered Johnny.

"As I was saying before I was so rudely interrupted, Harriet Tubman Carver, Riet," spoke Provenzano apparently losing interest in the intruder for the moment.

"Yeah, that's me, you mad motherfucker," she answered back, and Van looked at her in amazement. His mother had never used any word stronger than *darn*.

"So you thought that you could screw a white guy and get away it? Well, OK, this is New York, and the fucking pinko liberals believe that it's just fine. You know, there is no KKK here . . . unfortunately. So, you see, it isn't the fact that you screwed a white man. You just happened to screw the *wrong* white man."

"I loved him," responded Riet, " . . . and he loved me." She turned to Van and said with tears in her eyes, "And that's the truth." Van just nodded. "So, you can go to hell, you freaking bastard."

"No, you can call me Mad Guy. I've grown to like the name, and it's you who's got to go." He lowered the gun at Riet's head and closed one eye as if he was about to aim and shoot. Riet tensed, and both Van and Johnny prepared to spring into motion. With an evil laugh, Guy pulled the gun back to his chest.

"Or I could go back to my original plan, the one that I had before Mr. Jack Paradise decided to get involved. Is that even your real name?"

"No, it's Jacob Paradowski," answered Jack, lying merely for the sake of annoying Provenzano.

"Oh, a Jew bastard to boot."

"It's Polish, if you really care."

"No, I don't care. Now open the cooler on the right side of the deck. Not the left. That is where the champagne that I so graciously offered to my guests is held."

"Why should I do anything you ask?" shot back Johnny.

"Because if you don't, I will put a bullet in your head immediately. If you listen, you may be able to stall for time and figure out a way to take me down. Now, as I was saying before I was so rudely interrupted . . . Open that cooler and take out what's inside." Johnny found two pairs of handcuffs.

"Now cuff the bitch and her *oreo* son to the railings on each side of the deck," said Mad Guy as he aimed the gun at Johnny's head with the threat of a bullet implied. Having no choice, Johnny did as told. He allowed himself to hope that securing Riet meant that he was going to let them live. Why cuff them if you were just going to put a bullet in them very soon?

"Done," said Johnny after he had placed one ring around each rail and then hooked the ring on one rail to Riet's right wrist and the ring on the other rail to Van's left wrist.

"Let me see your handiwork, Mr. Paradowski. Riet, Van, let me see your wrists." As both of them raised their one cuffed hand, Provenzano screamed in rage, "I wanted you to cuff both hands around each rail."

"You know us Pollocks," answered Johnny without a smile on his face.

"I should have you come over here and get these keys, and have you fix what you screwed up." He pointed down to a hook on the wall of the lower deck just below his dangling feet.

"I'll . . ." started Johnny but was immediately cut off by the maniac who had just realized that he would be inviting his prisoner a little too close to where he was sitting.

"Stay put . . . and sorry, no jewelry for you," remarked Guy. "I was only expecting two until you invited yourself to my party."

"My mama always told me that a good host should always prepare for extra guests," replied Johnny displaying a false bravado. He understood that it soon would not matter. He was going to be the first victim.

"I had this grand plan, which I thought incredibly generous of me. I was just going to have the *oreo* superstar's legs broken. You know make him a cripple. That was why I needed to see him tonight. Tomorrow, he has his physical for the Mets. Until Giovanni Junior passes that, he has nothing. My timing was impeccable."

"You bastard," screamed the furious Riet who now lurched forward only to be restrained by her shackles.

"Fuck you, you prick," yelled Van standing tall and proud, but not wanting to give Provenzano the pleasure of seeing him struggle.

Johnny stood in the middle of the mother and son. He said nothing. The gun was pointed directly at his head, holding him in his place as well as any physical constraint could ever accomplish. He looked from side to side, looking for something to get him back in the game. Anything.

"The best part is that Miss Carver here wouldn't say a word, or I would have her, and her little *oreo* wiped out. She would have to live every day of her life wondering what great things would have happened if someone hadn't screwed it up. It would've been fun. Don't ya think?"

"You evil scumbag," now it was Johnny's turn to start to lose his temper.

"You, Mr. Paradise or Paradowski, screwed up those plans because you showed up. I could have counted on these two keeping silent to protect their lives. But you are a messy detail that I would always have to worry about."

"Stop! Why are you doing this?" Riet screamed, tears running down her cheeks. "They were just kids in a band trying to make something of themselves."

"And I was just a young man trying to make something of *myself*," screamed Guy in a bellowing voice that filled the entire boat, "And then your asshole boyfriend screwed me. He was asked point blank if the band was legal. The cocksucker lied. I had the phone records checked, and the call went to his house. The Cat would have checked these things out. I knew him."

"Before you killed him!" Johnny surprised himself by blurting out this unknown bit of information. Guy's eyes squinted in confusion and disbelief. Only three people knew about his midnight visit to the Driftwood, and this guy wasn't one of them. "Gio never took that call to his house from Vinnie the Cat."

"Liar, you couldn't know that unless . . ."

"Unless I was there."

"And?"

"I was there," whispered Johnny in a barely audible voice, his head bowed in a moment of penance that had long been coming in his life. It had been building from the first time he heard of the death of his friends one by one. Gio's death had sucked him into a vortex of pain. He would not allow another death to happen while he stood silently. He lifted his head from his chest and stared directly into the eyes of the man he had hated almost as long as he had hated himself. No more whispers, no more lies. His voice boomed out, "I was there. It was me who talked to Vinnie the Cat."

"How?"

"I'm Johnny Cipp."

"Johnny Cipp . . . fuckin' Johnny Cipp. After all these years." A smile broke across his face. "After so long and so much searching, I've got you right here on my boat."

"I took that call. I'm the one who lied to Vinnie the Cat. You had no reason to kill all the others. There is no need to kill *them*," he said turning and pointing to Riet and Van.

"You don't understand. You have given me such joy, Johnny Fuckin' Cipp. What do the shrinks say nowadays? You've given me closure. Yeah, killing you is going to give me closure."

"But there is no reason to hurt them," pleaded Johnny as Mad Guy started to laugh uncontrollably.

"You don't get it. Now they're just collateral damage, like so many other pieces of shit that got in my way. In fact, I think it'll be more fun to kill them first and let you watch. That way you can feel even more guilt on your way to hell." Van and Riet pulled at their chains, hoping at least to get close enough to die together.

"No," screamed Johnny.

"Johnny Cipp, Johnny Cipp, do you dare give me orders?" bellowed Mad Guy at the top of his lungs. At the same time, he raised his gun and aimed at Van. "My alternate plan was to shoot out both of the kid's kneecaps. I always wondered if I could make that shot. I think I'll do that first. You know, just to see." He raised the gun and pointed it at Van's left kneecap. Johnny knew that Provenzano was done playing with them. This time he would shoot.

"Please, don't," pleaded Johnny.

"Beg, Johnny Cipp, beg," roared the uncontrollable voice. He stood up on the flybridge extending to his full height. Air filled his lungs and increased the volume of his wailing voice, and again he screamed out even louder, "Beg, Johnny Cipp, beg."

"Johnny?" a soft voice spoke behind Guy's back. However, no one heard the whisper. It was quieter than even the sound of the silenced gun that had just been fired.

A small red spot appeared on Johnny's abdomen as the bullet drove him back into Van's waiting arms. It was not long before the crimson stain started to spread into a broad rosette on his pale blue Margaritaville t-shirt.

"Oops," said Provenzano and followed it with a riotous laugh. Because of the height difference between Johnny and Van, the shot meant for Van's knee had caught Johnny much higher up on his torso as he moved in front of the young athlete. Johnny moved his hand to his wound and realized from the blood that he was not in good shape. He raised his eyes to the maniac who now played out a scenario he thought to be humorous. Blowing on the top of the gun, he then pretended to replace the Glock in a fictional holster on his right hip.

"He always was an asshole," Johnny said only loud enough for Van to hear. This was not because he was afraid that Guy would overhear him, but rather because the bullet was taking its toll. He could barely raise his voice.

"Johnny?" again the voice behind the madman spoke.

"Shut up, retard," was the impatient response as Guy turned to Tony. He was incredulous as he glared at him. "You don't speak for twenty years, and the first thing you say is 'Johnny'?"

———————◆———————

"Push me," said Johnny in a barely audible whisper.

"What? Are you crazy?" answered Van with a confused expression on his face.

"Push me towards him. Trust me on this."

"When?"

"Now, while he is distracted." With that, Van propelled Johnny toward his certain death. To Johnny, it seemed as if time had been suspended. The seven-foot gap that would lead to the ladder looked miles away. Moreover, when he got there, he knew that he still would not be able to reach Provenzano who was above the deck on the flybridge. As he staggered forward, he started to lose consciousness. He was rapidly losing blood. Still, he went on. In his weakened state, his mind kept replaying a scene from his childhood. He was back in his room recreating a heroic feat. He knew this time, however, it was for real.

Into the valley of death rode the six hundred.

He would be like Errol Flynn in *The Charge of the Light Brigade*. He wasn't in the British army, and there weren't 599 others with him, but this *was* a suicide mission. He would finally be the hero he had imagined so many times in his youth. A smile crossed his face as his illusion continued.

Theirs was not to reason why,
Theirs was but to do or die.

Yeah, he was pretty sure that he was going to die, but hey, he had been given twenty-three free years. He understood the concept of living on borrowed time. Time to pay back the loan. Time to pay the reaper. He heard nothing as Guy's second shot had caught him in his left thigh. And still, he staggered toward his goal. He knew where he wanted to go.

Onward, into the Valley of Death.

Johnny strode forward until he hit the wall of the enclosed galley of the *Fun Ghoul*. There he turned and faced Van and Riet, and with a slight grin on his face, slid down the wall until his buttocks came to rest on the floor. Above him, the path of his descent down the wall was marked in a trail of his blood.

"Yoo-hoo, you under there," mocked Mad Guy as he now lay prone on the flybridge floor and peered over the edge of the overhang. He was confident that Johnny was a done deal. When he saw the blood on the wall and floor all around him, he began to celebrate.

"End of story. Case closed. I win!" Mad Guy began a ridiculous dance on the flybridge floor directly above where Johnny sat bleeding profusely. The light that shined from the boat's floodlights cast eerie shadows against the back of the cockpit as the lunatic danced something vaguely resembling an Italian tarantula dance.

Van and Riet looked away from the maniac's dance at the bleeding figure of Johnny illuminated by a floodlight right over his head. His right hand lay in a balled fist, and his legs splayed forward. His head drooped, and he resembled a drunk who was sleeping off a binge. They wondered if he was still breathing. Van stretched his left hand across the void between his mother and him. She met his hand with hers. Their fingertips touched, and this was their only success in consoling each other. They saw Johnny's fate, and they knew theirs would be the same.

"Don't die on me, Just Jack. I still have so much to learn from you," yelled Van across the void that separated them. Riet cried. Then Johnny opened his eyes. A small smile came across his face. Johnny's face seemed to be trying to send a silent message to the shackled pair as his eyes went from staring straight at them to down at his right hand. He repeated this ritual until he saw that he had their attention. When he knew they were looking at his balled-up fist, he suddenly opened it to reveal small silver keys to the handcuffs that bound the mother and son. After he had been shot the second time he had spotted the keys and their elaborate Italian flag keychain and had staggered in its direction. He collapsed only after his prize was firmly in his grasp. The question now was if he could get them to Van before he lost consciousness.

"Well, it's your turn to die," said Mad Guy turning his attention back to Riet and Van.

———◆———

"Those Born Free! How ironic that the last two to die won't be so free. Get it? Not so free!"

"We've been free for more than a hundred years, you stupid ass honky," screamed the now livid Van.

"Oh, that's a good one. I was thinking not free because you're handcuffed. But, hey, I like your take on it even better. You know you two being *coons* and all." Van pulled at his chained wrist so hard that Riet was afraid he would tear his arm off and Provenzano jumped up and down in joy.

"Those Born Free. I love the irony," he screamed one more time at the top of his lungs.

"Those Born Free?" said the weak voice behind him.

"I told you to shut up, you fucking retard," said Mad Guy and he raised his hand as if to hit his brother. As Tony flinched, Guy again laughed heartily. Johnny had been waiting for a distraction. With every ounce of strength he could muster, he raised his right arm and hurled the keys toward Van. At first, the young athlete seemed lost. The floodlight over Johnny's head shone in his eyes, and he lost sight of the flight of the keychain. Suddenly, Van raised his one free hand to block the light while focusing on the path of the key. Soon the instrument of their freedom was in his hand.

"You taught me well, Coach," whispered Van across the expanse of the deck. Van unlocked his wrist and passed the keys to his mother who did likewise. Now, however, they were at a loss as to what to do with their newfound freedom and so kept the illusion of restraint a while longer as Guy turned back to them.

Johnny tried to move, but blood loss had weakened him. Still, he knew that he had to join the battle one last time. He had to create a diversion to allow Van and Riet to escape. He had no way of knowing that neither could swim and there were no life jackets in sight. It would be just like this idiot Provenzano not to have them on a boat that was now six miles from the nearest shoreline. He didn't know what Van and Riet would do once he diverted the attention of their demented captor, but he had to try.

"Tony, I'm going to beat the crap out of you if so much as

turn around again. Understand?"

Tony. That's who's up there, thought Johnny. He placed one hand on the second rung of the ladder that led to the fly-bridge. As Guy resumed a sitting position facing the captive mother and son, his feet once again dangled from this perch location. He was truly enjoying himself. Guy couldn't see Johnny tucked under the overhanging area. He assumed that two bullets had been enough to finish off the last of his problems. Johnny, however, could see Guy's legs and they beckoned to him as a ray of hope. If he could just reach one of the legs and pull the bastard down, Van could probably join in the fight before Guy could use his gun. It wasn't a great plan, but it was a plan. And so, Johnny began to climb. Johnny doubted he had the strength to mount the ladder's first rung, no less to reach high enough to grab the luna-tic who threatened the lover and son of his best friend. He closed his eyes and began his task. As he did so, he sang to himself softly. So long ago that same voice had been play-fully mocked by his friends. Nevertheless, they loved him, and he loved them as brothers and from that knowledge he drew his strength.

Suddenly I turn around,
And all is lost,
There is no turning back,
Once that line's been crossed.

Johnny placed his left hand on the third rung of the ladder and pulled his weight up from the floor. His left leg rebelled in pain, and he fell back to a sitting position. He hoped that he had not brought attention to himself. He moved his uninjured leg into a kneeling position and tried again. This time he moved his right hand to the fourth rung. Now came the test. Could he hold his weight entirely with his

arms? The pain continued to course through his weak and
blood-starved muscles, but he knew he had no choice. He
had deserted the fight once before in his life, and it had
destroyed every feeling inside him. He now wrapped his
left arm around the third rung and put the pressure of his
weight on it as he reached with his right arm to an even
higher level.

He felt his consciousness leaving him. Not enough blood
was getting to the brain. Looking down at the puddle of red
below him, he wondered if there was still enough circulat-
ing in his entire body to feed the brain that he had for so
long abused. *Just hold on a little longer.* He lost touch with the
real world around him, concentrating on merely the next
obstacle that he needed to overcome. He thought that he
heard the voices of Gio, Jimmy Mac, Bracko and Tinman
singing along with him. They were pushing him from their
graves. One more rung.

> *Fear of things that have gone,*
> *And who I've always been.*
> *Fear of what I'll never be,*
> *Fear I'll never win.*

The entire group had embraced "The Thief of My Forever" and made it a tale of all their lives. Now only Johnny
was left alive to be haunted by its meaning. As he pushed
upward, it was the final verse that reverberated in his head
. . .

> *In time, TIME takes everything,*
> *As memories fade to never,*
> *How long will he steal from me?*
> *This thief of my forever.*

———

"Time to die, *oreo*," taunted Provenzano and he lowered the gun and took aim at Van. "Then you, *whoo-a*," he said, motioning to Riet.

"Put that gun down and see how big you are then," Van screamed back. Every bit of his willpower was concentrated on keeping his unshackled hand hidden until he saw the right opportunity to literally play his hand.

"And the story will finally be over. Revenge is sweet. Those kids fucked me, and now they and everyone around them will be dead. It just shows that you don't mess with Guy Provenzano."

"Isn't that *Mad Guy* Provenzano?"

"Tough talk from someone whose nickname is Angel, you faggot."

Van glared at him. He waited for the right moment. Could he reach down and possibly grab the champagne bottle in the cooler and use it as a weapon?

Johnny's hand reached the top rung, and he held on for dear life. He wrapped his left arm around the ladder with his elbow using all its strength to hold his weight. He started to lose consciousness again, the lack of blood continuing to take its toll. He now lay helpless within full view of Provenzano . . . if the madman were to look down to his right.

"You know what else you are? A *mule*. Do you know what a mule is? It's the product of a jackass and a horse screwing." The more he taunted Van, the more he leveled the gun at the younger man's heart. "You have some pure Italian blood coursing through your veins. Unfortunately, it is mixed with that jackass nigger blood of that bitch. So, mule it is."

Van searched for something, anything that he could use as a weapon. Without giving away his free right hand, he realized that the only item available to him were the handcuffs

themselves that had bound him. When the time was right
. . .

"So *oreo*, or *mule*, it really doesn't matter, you're going to
die now. It will finally be over."

"So, you admit that you killed all the others in the band?"
Riet stared into his eyes with hatred.

"You say 'admit it' like I should be ashamed. I not only
killed all those pricks who screwed me, but their family
members every time it was convenient. The kid from the
candy store and his father . . . that kid at college and his parents . . . the kid with the weird name. What was it?"

"Bracko!" yelled Riet.

*"Bracko?" whispered the faint voice sitting in the chair away from
the action. For the first time in years, Tony's eyes showed some rec-
ognition, some understanding.*

"And, of course, there was Gio. He was the most fun. I
did the old schoolyard lynching on him. And years later,
when no one would make the connection, I took care of his
parents just for fun. Yeah, *mule*, that's why you are short one
set of grandparents."

"Gio," whimpered Riet and hung her head.

Seeing the pain this caused, Guy continued to taunt her.
"Yeah, killing Gio was the most fun of them all. I was there
for it."

"Gio," whispered Riet.

Van turned to look at his distraught mother. Now was the
time to act before he had to listen to any more bullshit or
see his mother hurt.

*"Gio dead?" said Tony in a more powerful voice than he had used
in years. He began to stir from his favorite seat.*

The cacophony of voices brought Johnny back to consciousness. His train of thought continued from the last memory that had rambled through his mind. Now there was clarity.

The Thief of My Forever wasn't anything abstract like time, brutality, or hopelessness. The Thief of My Forever was real. He is real. He stands only inches away from me. This bastard took the lives of my friends, and you can't get any more forever than that. He's the goddamn thief.

"And, of course, last but not least, I finally got Johnny Cipp. I kept holding off taking out his parents, hoping he would contact them. And then they had the balls to die of natural causes."

"Johnny?" Tony rose from his seat.

"So *mule* or *oreo*, whichever you prefer, it all ends here," said Mad Guy, distracted for the briefest of moments by the stirring behind him. It was enough time for Van to act.

"It's not *mule* or *oreo*! It's Giovanni DeAngelis, Junior," screamed Van as he began his charge at Mad Guy. Simultaneously, he hurled the newly loosened handcuffs directly at Guy's head. They were not much of a weapon, but he hoped that at least they would divert Guy's attention long enough for him to make a decent charge at the flybridge. He was wrong. Guy was able to avoid the accurately thrown cuffs by dropping to his knees and ducking under the assault.

"You prick," bellowed Mad Guy as he stood up and attempted to lift the Glock to fire at the charging athlete. However, even as his body rose to most of his full height, his right arm was prevented from being lifted. He looked down in horror as the bloody hand of Johnny Cipp held firmly to his right wrist. While dodging the thrown cuffs, he put himself within reach of a semi-conscious hand that now clutched and restrained him with every ounce of strength remaining in his body.

"It ends when, I say it ends, Thief," whispered Johnny.

"Or it ends when I kill you!" Though Johnny held his wrist and prevented him from aiming the weapon, Guy's trigger finger remained engaged. He fired. The bullet struck the side of Johnny's head. Weakened by this final trauma, he fell from the ladder and landed forcefully on the hard deck. He didn't move.

"Johnny," screamed Riet, "You killed Johnny." Van's charge was stopped in its tracks as the gun now rose from Mad Guy's side and was aimed directly at him.

"You kill Johnny! You kill Gio! You kill Bracko!" screeched Tony as he lumbered toward his brother.

With that, Guy turned his head away from Van and towards his brother. Tears rolled down Tony's face as he threw both arms around Guy and crushed him into immobility. The older Provenzano still had use of his wrist. Guy lifted the Glock and started to fire into his brother's midsection and still Tony held on.

"No! No!" yelled the panicked Mad Guy as he realized that his wounded brother continued to hold tight and was now moving forward toward the starboard side of the boat. He fired again only to hear the blank clicking of an empty gun. Still holding his brother tightly, Tony continue to push to the edge of the flybridge until the two interlocked bodies plunged over the side into the deep dark waters of the Long Island Sound.

Guy struggled against the unmovable hold of his brother's arms. Deeper and deeper they descended. As the final breaths left their lungs, they remained intertwined with the elder brother's face a study in fear. In sharp contrast, Tony's mouth revealed a faint smile. Gone were the horrors that he had tried to escape with drugs. Gone was the ridicule of all who saw him in the street. Gone was the pain. Gone were foggy memories of a tragic life. For only one brief time in his entire existence, he felt happiness. A mind that understood very little had realized his brother had taken away the people who had given him joy.

As they sank into the silent depths from which they would never return, Tony's mind and body welcomed a release from the misery of a life he had ceased wanting to live decades before.

Tony was free at last.

PART
5

"Time Is Here and Gone"
– The Doobie Brothers

23

The Other Side of Life:
"Long Time Gone"
– Crosby, Stills, and Nash

**February
2013**

H E STARED AT THE WORN composition book that lay
on the passenger seat of his two-year-old Nissan
Altima. He hadn't seen it since 1990, but he knew what
he needed to do with it now. Thus, he began the scenic, but emotional southbound trek along the Overseas
Highway of the Florida Keys.

As he approached Key Largo, his eyes watered slightly.
He loved going down to Key West to visit, but this time
his mission was clouded by sadness. He could not enjoy the
glistening waters that surrounded him on both sides as the
Everglades gave way to islands of the Upper Keys. Without
taking his eyes from the majestic view of the Seven Mile
Bridge, he placed his hand down on the seat beside him and
caressed the book that had so changed his life on that dra-
matic weekend so long ago.

He had not seen it since that night. His mother Riet had

tenderly put it away in the bottom drawer of her antique dresser. There were nights when he heard sobbing behind her bedroom door and instinctively knew that she was either re-reading the contents of its pages or just holding it to her bosom and reminiscing. But, that was over now. His mother had passed away after a long and painful battle with breast cancer. She had died after living a little over 64 wonderful years. Her son and her husband Earl had been at her side. She had married Van's agent and lawyer after a courtship begun in the chaos of that weekend in June over two decades before. Van had not seen that romance coming. It had taken months for Earl to gain his mother's trust. She had to be sure that he had not been a pawn of Guy Provenzano from the beginning. It had worked out, and Earl and Riet had happily grown old together. . .until cancer struck.

Earl and Van had comforted each other through the long nights of vigil by her bedside and become closer than ever. Van had already loved the man, or at least appreciated him. Earl had taken the majority of Van's signing bonus money and invested wisely for his stepson. Earl had investigated and researched companies for the boy and then bought and sold stock at just the right times. Through the 1990s and on into the present day, Earl had talked about Apple and Google as if they were oil wells discovered in his backyard. They might have well been for the amount of money that had accumulated in Van's Fidelity account. For all his efforts, Earl refused to take a penny in commission for himself.

Earl and Riet Ruffin continued to live in the same house on Colfax Street in Cambria Heights until the very end of her time. More and more it became *their* house and less and less the house that had been a part of so many memories from the 1960s. As her love and respect for Earl grew with every passing moment, Riet's thoughts of Gio faded. They never entirely passed into oblivion. "The book" still made its way out of the dresser drawer occasionally and gave solace to its owner. Now that would never happen again.

Thus, Van's task was clear. He needed to return the book to its rightful home. His journey was now nearing its conclusion. He had navigated the first 90 miles of the scenic drive without enjoying the actual scenes as much as he usually did. His mind had been too engrossed in the past. He often came down here to vacation with his children. He tried to think of those happier times now and somehow defeat the gloominess that had enveloped his trip so far. He returned to reality as he crossed the bridge from Cudjoe Key onto Sugarloaf Key. He hardly noticed the fishermen with their lines cast over the side of the bridge. Many times in the past, he had stopped here with the kids, to drop a line or two himself. His wife Kim would chide him that they needed to get going, but he knew she enjoyed the brief stopovers as much as he did. Today, however, was different. Despite her offer to join him on his travels, he had chosen to do this alone. He would not make any stops. That had been what he had promised himself until . . .

The Sugarloaf School loomed around the next bend in the road, and he couldn't resist the temptation to stop. Sure, he had been here many times since his days as a player for his college team. In fact, in a few weeks, he would be right back down on this same field again with a bat in hand, hitting grounders and fly balls to *his* team. When Cal Fremont had retired three years ago, Van accepted the position as his replacement. He loved the job and was glad that all those years ago the coach insisted they all take the student part of the student-athlete title seriously. Van was now a college instructor as well as a coach. His life had become all he could have asked for when his major league baseball career came to an abrupt end.

The Mets had been patient and intelligent with his devel-

opment as a player in their system. While the media and
fans had screamed for his major league debut to save the
franchise that had fallen on poor times, the Mets waited
until he had honed his craft in the minors for two years.
Van "The Angel" DeAngelis finally made it to the "Show"
in April of 1992. For the first six weeks of the season he was
batting over .300 and had blasted seven home runs. It was
a good start. However, these were also the final statistics
of the young player's career. On a sunny day in mid-May,
Van had pursued a long fly ball that most outfielders would
never dream of reaching. His raw speed and athleticism had
tracked down and corralled the prospective extra-base hit.
A second later, his momentum would carry him into the
ivy-covered left field brick wall of Chicago's Wrigley Field,
resulting in a severe concussion. The medical staff took him
off the field on a gurney. It did not end there. The doctors
warned that any other injury of the same sort in the future
could result in permanent brain damage. Though distraught,
Van recovered due to the love of his mother, stepfather, and
his budding romance with Kim Mason. Gone was the angry
young man that had taunted Just Jack on this very field in
1990.

Van DeAngelis took up the Mets' offer of a scouting position and used his free time to earn a graduate degree in
health and sports medicine. Eventually, he left professional
baseball entirely for the world of college teaching and coaching. With his dream of superstardom gone, he realized he
could be content following in Cal Fremont's footsteps. As
a bonus, his new career gave him a more stable lifestyle in
which he and Kim could raise Giovanni III, John Earl, and
Harriet Callie.

"Nico" showed promise as an athlete like his father. Kim
and Van reasoned that both the "Gio" and the "Van" part
of the name Giovanni had been used and that only left the

last syllable. Thus, the oldest of three became Ni and eventually Nico. When someone pointed out to the couple that John was the English translation of the Italian Giovanni and therefore they had given their two sons the same name, they just smiled. "The two of them were and are that close," was the standard reply. No one got the inside joke. Both John Earl and Harriet Callie showed a propensity and an interest in music and the professional lessons had already begun for both of them.

Yes, life was good for Van, and it all began here on Sugarloaf Key one afternoon over two decades ago. He parked the car, got out and walked to the chain link fence that surrounded the field. Spring practices had begun the second week in February for the local high school team. He knew Coach Cronshaw well since they shared an area when he continued the tradition of spring break practices in the Keys. He did not have the time today to visit with the coach, but he would be back soon, and the two of them would go out for dinner. Today was about reliving the past, not looking into the future. He smiled as he remembered his first run in with "Just Jack" and how it had changed him before he even understood his connection to the man and the man's journal. He walked back to his car just as one of the high school players lost a fly ball in the sun.

"Use that glove hand to shield your eyes," he heard Coach Cronshaw scream to the fifteen-year-old who had almost been beaned by the wayward ball.

"That a way, coach," Van said under his breath and lowered himself into the driver's seat of the Altima. He again rubbed his hand over the worn book on the seat next to him. "You're going home now."

He crossed over the bridge from Boca Chica and was finally on the island of Key West. He traveled down Truman Avenue until it ran into Duval Street. It was then that he realized that he was too early for his appointment and diverted his car toward Smathers Beach. There he could kill some time. He got out of his vehicle and took his beach chair from its trunk. He walked across Roosevelt Street and through the cut out in the dunes and finally onto the sand. He placed the Tommy Bahama chair in the sand facing out into the Atlantic.

He took off his shoes and let his toes enjoy the feeling of the soft white sand falling in between them. He would wait out the two or so hours until his 6 p.m. dinner appointment. He looked out into the bright sky and calm blue waters. And thought back to the night so long ago on the water . . .

24

The Other Side of Life:
"Knockin' on Heaven's Door"
- Eric Clapton version

M AD GUY HAD MET HIS end thanks in large part to
Tony's sacrifice and Johnny's bravery. After Riet
and Van felt the relief of knowing that they were not
going to die, they were brought back to reality by the
sight of Johnny's crumpled body on the ship's deck. He
had taken three bullets in his effort to save them. As
they ran to him, they feared the worst. As they bent over
to determine if he was breathing, they were not only
shocked by the fact that he spoke but also, what he said.

"I guess that neither one of you has ever piloted a boat,"
rasped the fading voice of Johnny.

"Neither one of us has ever even been on a boat," answered
Riet.

"And so, the adventure continues," replied the fallen man
as a faint smile crossed his lips. Riet knelt behind Johnny
and rested his upper body against her chest. As Johnny whispered instructions to her, she relayed them up to Van who
had taken up command in the captain's chair on the flybridge. With time and patience, the Fun Ghoul found its

way to land on the north shore of Long Island. They tied
up to the dock at a marina that had closed for the night and
did not have any security similar to that of the marina they
left behind in Flushing. Van carried Johnny off the boat and
laid him on the dock, and Riet explained to the two of them
that she would call an ambulance from a pay phone.

"No," responded Johnny in the loudest voice he could
muster. "They can't tie you and Van to me, the boat, or
Guy."

"But, you're bleeding to death." said the shocked Riet.

"Maybe, but, I think that I can hold out a little bit longer.
Van, start the engine and then wedge a flashlight into the
steering wheel. Send the boat directly out into the sound.
Eventually, the waves will knock the flashlight from the
wheel, and it will fall. There will be no evidence where this
boat came from. Then carry me as far away from here as
you are able." He turned to Riet, "Only then, can you call
anonymously to report a victim you came upon."

"We're not leaving you . . . . after all that you have done.
You don't deserve that."

"If you and Van are here, you'll have an awful lot of
explaining to do. Not good for you. Not good for me.
Remember we don't know who in Guy's gang will know or
care what happened to him. We don't know who will want
revenge. And what of Van's career?"

"How about you let me decide that," interrupted Van. "I
don't run from anyone."

"Well, bravery is not what it is cracked up to be," Johnny
replied with a soft smile and used his index finger to point in
turn to each of his three wounds. "Besides, there is no way
for the police to identify me or tie any of us to this." He was
lying, of course. His blood was all over the Fun Ghoul, and
it would not take much to match it to the John Doe found
not too far from the waterfront. However, Van and Riet

would be long gone by then.

Van carried Johnny about a half a mile and lay him down on the corner of the street that none of them recognized because they had no working knowledge of this exclusive section of Nassau County. Meanwhile, Riet found a pay phone and called anonymously for help. As they reluctantly left him sitting alone and started to retreat into the shadows, they heard him making soft unintelligible sounds. Was he talking to himself? Was that singing they heard?

"I knew you wouldn't fail me, Music Doctor. You're still here until the end . . ."

He struggled to breathe as blood flowed from his three wounds.

"Yes, that is a perfect song . . . so perfect. . . I wondered what song you would pick when I finally made things right. . . what would be the sound of my redemption."

He lifted his hand from the wound in his abdomen and held it to his eyes. Damn, that ain't a good sign, he thought to himself.

". . . And, yeah, I know, the song isn't just for me. . . it's for Tony too. I think that he is finally at peace in Long Island Sound. Shit, Music Doctor, you are so damn ironic, and you have a sense of humor too! I asked what my sound of redemption would be and you took it quite literally."

He coughed up flecks of blood that spewed out of his mouth and on to his chin.

"Rest in peace, Tony, rest in peace. The Music Doctor is singing to us, and he picked just the right song . . ."

Hello, Darkness, my old friend,
I've come to talk with you again.

"We've got to go help him," said Riet frantically. Van had just started out of their hiding place when they heard the closing sounds of sirens . . . and Johnny's fading voice.

". . . echoed the sounds of silence."

25

The Other Side of Life:
"With a Little Help from My Friends"
- *The Beatles*

RIET AND VAN KEPT A close watch on Johnny until they heard the sirens of the approaching paramedics. They stayed in hiding as instructed. They tried to see if Johnny had made it, but could learn nothing from the actions of the paramedics. When he was loaded for transport, were they still trying to save him or was that a shroud that had been placed over his head?

After the ambulance had faded into the night, Riet had gone into her bag and removed the slip of paper that had been handed to her two days before by Maria. She knew of this woman only from the journal and their brief meeting. She could only pray that the person described had not changed with time. She was not disappointed.

Maria had dropped everything and driven to Van and Riet. Her prompt arrival had prevented the mother and son from trying to make a public homeward journey while soaked in Johnny's blood. When she left them off at home, all three seemed to be asking the same important question. What now? Maria rushed back to her place in bed before her husband ever woke up for his 8 a.m. to 4 p.m. shift. Riet and Van washed up and quickly disposed of the clothes that remained evidence of their involvement. There was no sleep for any of the three that night, or for the next few days.

At 8 a.m., Earl Ruffin knocked on the door of Riet's house. He could wait no longer to find out what had happened the night before. He had known the woman only a few months but had already come to think of her as more of a friend than a client. His time with Richie Shea had given him a bad feeling about what was going on, and he could not wait any longer to get Riet's take on the overall situation. When Van answered the door, he had no idea how to react to this new arrival. Was this lawyer in on it from the beginning, or had he been bought off later on down the line?

"C'mon in," said Riet pushing Van aside. It was apparent to Van that his mother did not in the slightest bit share his fears. In fact, was it Van's imagination or was his mother just a little too friendly with this Mr. Ruffin? Something either spoken or unspoken was going on between these two.

There was a bit of a feeling out process before Riet and Van decided to level with Earl Ruffin. When the time was right, Riet went into her bedroom and opened the dresser drawer that would be home to the journal for the next two decades. She removed the book, walked into the living room, and placed the journal on the lawyer's lap. For the next hour, Riet and Earl ran through an abridged version of the journal, only covering the parts that Ruffin would need to see to understand the situation. When that task was completed, she relayed the harrowing events of the night before.

When it was all over, he sat dumbfounded. He had to consider not only what had happened to Riet, but also his experience the night before. Richie Shea seemed to be distracted all night as if he was waiting for something to happen. Shea was conflicted about what to do next. Earl had no way of knowing that Shea had been told not to take action until he had spoken to Guy. In the end, he just dropped Earl off and said goodbye. Now it was Earl's turn to be indecisive. Was he their lawyer or their friend? In the end, his inner sense of morals won out over his responsibilities as a member of the New York State Bar, and he decided to join the conspiracy.

"I've tried all my contacts, and no one seems to know what happened to Johnny. Even if he is alive, he has big problems. By law, the doctors would have to report any gunshot victims to the police. There is a pretty good chance that Johnny would become a very public figure. And if he . . . "

"No, he just can't be dead," pined Riet.

"I don't know. I just don't know."

Maria called each morning to see if Riet or Earl had found out about Johnny's fate, but the couple had no answers to give.

At the end of the third day, Johnny, unconscious but living body, appeared on a stretcher at Riet's doorstep.

———◆———

Johnny had had his wounds professionally tended to and was on a very long road to recovery. But how had he gotten there? Riet took him in without question and found a room in her home for him to heal. What followed were days of recurrent unconsciousness. Even when conscious, Johnny would reveal nothing about how he had arrived in the Heights. He never would.

When Maria called for an update, Riet had invited her over to assist in nursing Johnny back to health. While her husband was at work and her kids at summer camp, Maria made several trips to the Heights to give Riet the assistance she needed. At first, Johnny had not been aware of her presence and therefore did not see her emotional collapse the first time that she set eyes on him. Eventually, Van knew that the two of them had had emotional talks in the privacy of Johnny's room.

Van also watched his mother and Maria grow closer over their shared burden. He observed them separately and jointly taking care of Johnny. They changed his bandages, fixed his bed, washed him down, and administered some over-the-counter medication. In the end, he saw them laugh together. He remembered the section of the journal where Johnny had fantasized about the future. If things had been different perhaps, the families would have been having those barbeques together. Perhaps after dinner, Gio and Johnny would be playing and singing together.

Eventually, Johnny had gotten well enough to be driven back down to his home. Van drove Johnny's car down while Riet and Earl followed carefully behind him with Johnny stretched out in the back seat. In Florida, Van left Johnny to report to his minor league assignment. Riet and Earl continued to Key West where they stayed for a few more weeks caring for Johnny. They then drove home at the end of the summer.

Riet never returned to see Johnny again. She feared that perhaps she would be followed and therefore put Johnny in danger. Johnny would never return to New York and he never did explain why. However, they often talked on the phone and communicated through Van.

Conversely, Van had come back often to see his father's friend. Just Jack had been good to him and Johnny saved his life. Not being able to decide whether to call him Jack or Johnny, he settled on "J." When his own kids came along, "Uncle J's" place became the destination of many family trips.

Van looked out at the water and noticed that the sun had disappeared and darkness was now encompassing the beach. A little more than a mile away the massive crowds that had lined the docks at Mallory Square had toasted a celebratory farewell to the sun's final rays of light. This ceremony was a ritual celebrated 365 days a year, weather permitting. Even when clouds blackened the sky, a certain percentage of drunken key-wasted could be expected to show up anyway; never much caring if the sun made an appearance that day. Van knew this was the cue to take the book to its final destination.

26

Journal of Johnny Cipp

Entry # 108 – February 15, 2013

"Here in the Conch Republic"
-Howard Livingston and the Mile Marker 24 Band

IT HAS BEEN MORE THAN twenty-two years since my return to the Heights, and I haven't been back since. I can't go back. The events of 1967 and 1990 have never entirely left my waking thoughts. Each year I think about them less and less. All that changed today when this journal came back to me. All the emotions and feelings that I had relegated to the hidden recesses of my mind immediately flooded back. Van and I talked. We both felt the emotion of the moment.

I'd lost a band of friends in the 1960s, and I had duly mourned them in this journal and my life. As much as was humanly possible, this marble composition book and my writings in it had made me whole again. It had helped me cope with loss and guilt, and a myriad of other feelings that had consumed me for so long. In addition to the journal, I had the help of a cadre of new friends to get me through. I now had deep friendships with Cal and Van and their families, and I wouldn't want to leave out the compassion and friendship of Padre. I have them to help me live my life with hope and joy I'd never thought possible again. Now I have lost one of my new friends, and it hurts deeply. Van and I consoled each other long into the night, and then he left. I then took my old companion, this journal, back home.

I'm now sitting at my old desk. I've just opened the journal and looked at the last words that I wrote on that panicked afternoon in 1990. I'm indecisive about writing and reliving every moment that followed my decision to head North on that June morning. I think to myself *why*? This isn't my autobiography. I never meant for this book to portray a written record of all that has happened to me. I believe it has been the writing process itself that has been my salvation. As I have seen on t-shirts recently, "The Journey is the Destination." My journey with this book is nearly done.

I survived without this book's company for a long time and probably could've done so still if it hadn't found its way back to me. Now it feels like an old friend with whom I need to catch up. It calls to me to say something about my life and who I am now. I find that I'm breaking the one rule I made about this book . . . I am starting to write in the present tense. I will go on a little bit longer to honor the homecoming of the book, but that is all.

———◆———

No one ever connected any of us to the demise of Mad Guy. Well, almost no one. I find strange ironic pleasure in the fact that in the end, Provenzano suffered the same fate that he had given to Gio, a lonely water grave.

Entry #109

"Photographs and Memories"
– *Jim Croce*

As I page through the journal and recall the dark days that led me to write it, I think of how far I have come since then. My self-congratulations are interrupted by my discovery of two photos stuck in its wrinkled old pages, obviously for my benefit. As I look at these forgotten pictures, I can't help thinking of the old Jim Croce song "Photographs and Memories." I guess that the Music Doctor has returned with the book. I stop a minute to look at the two pictures that I haven't seen in decades.

The first photo, or should I say photos, are of Maria and me. They were taken in one of those photo kiosks that are found in amusement parks. The machine was set to take four consecutive pictures in a row of the subjects who had squeezed themselves in a tiny light proof booth. They are the only pictures ever taken of Maria and me. I remember her placing them in her pocket one of the last times I saw her in 1967. She must have carried them around for all these years?

In the first picture, our faces are full and facing the camera. I can see Maria's beauty radiating forward. The second and third images reveal us in various stages of preparing to kiss. The fourth picture needs no explanation. We took the opportunities where we found them in those days. It's the first picture that haunts me with thoughts of what might have been. I don't know how this strip made it into my journal. Did Maria leave them there while I recuperated at Riet's house long ago? Or were they a more recent edition given over to Riet or Van specifically for me to see now?

Maria, as far as I know, is still married with kids. In fact, she is probably a grandmother by now. I don't know. I haven't seen her since 1990 when . . .

She came almost every day to Riet's house during my recovery. For most of that time, I was barely conscious. At first, we didn't even talk. Toward the end of my stay, there were moments when we were alone, but we only stared at each other. What could I say to her? The old feelings had been rekindled in me, but she was now happily married. When it was decided that I would be leaving soon, Maria came in to be with me. Realizing it might be our final time together, we, at last, had a long talk. She broke the ice by mentioning that she'd seen Frank, my archrival for her affections. We laughed as she explained that he was now about three hundred pounds and as bald as a cue ball. I remember her saying, "I guess I made the right choice." She then realized what she'd said, and I saw tears form in her eyes. In the end, it hadn't been the right choice. I'd brought her years of pain and heartache. We sat and talked for about an hour that day and the years seemed to disappear. We were sixteen again and happy. The next day, Maria returned while I was sleeping and she left me a note.

Dear Johnny,
Good luck . . . and goodbye. I will always love you. I've read your journal, and I know what you have gone through. I hope that you understand that I'm happy now and that you should no longer feel any guilt about me. I have found my place in the sun. I am at peace. I am happy.
Maria

Placed on top of the note was the tiny silver band that I had inserted in the package I had sent to her. I hadn't meant it to be an invitation to rekindle our love or had I?

I had convinced myself that I was only letting her know I was now OK and that I had found my way. I guess she had reciprocated the feeling and laid the ring upon the note to let me know that she too was OK. I don't know why, but I still wear that ring on my pinkie. Now the 1967 pictures of Maria will find their final resting place in the journal. Perhaps someday I will look at them again. Probably not. *Photographs and memories.*

———◆———

The second photo carries my last secret with it. It's a story that I've never told anyone.

I remember very little of my first few days in the hospital. I floated through periods of unconsciousness and semi-consciousness. I became aware of the fact that I was being watched by a multitude of strange faces. I knew that they had a million questions for me, none of which I could answer. Therefore, I hid my improving alertness from them. That was until the third day. On that day, a tall, well-dressed man entered my room and signaled all the others to leave. The speed with which they were gone both impressed and frightened me. He flashed a badge at me that I didn't have time even to see.

"So, . . . I'm trying to figure out how the hell you killed Guy and got away with it," he said forcefully, but not belligerently. I stared at him as if he was speaking Martian. He continued. All the while my eyes remained more than half closed so I could claim to be out of it.

"Three of you go out on the boat with him and you end up in the hospital. Riet and Van end up safe and warm at home."

Holy shit, he knows their names!

"Ready to talk yet . . . Johnny . . . Johnny Cipp"

Like a reflex motion, my eyes flared open, and I saw a face that looked familiar. I knew him from that night. I strained my limited thought waves to place him.

"Richie . . . Richie Shea," the stranger said.

I'm dead, I think to myself.

"Guy's cousin," he followed.

Real, real dead.

"That's the bad news for you. The good news is that I don't give a flying fuck that you killed Guy. He was nuts, always was. He had me chasing you for twenty something years. I wasted an awful lot of energy doing my version of The Fugitive, and you were the good guy in the movie."

"So," I finally got up the nerve to speak, "where does that leave us?"

"Well, I think that I gotta kill Riet, Van, and that lawyer Ruffin, and of course, you."

Real, real, real dead. But then Shea smiles.

"Just kidding, trying on my cousin's shoes, so to speak. In reality, you did me a favor. Now I'm the boss. But I've got a little problem."

"And?" I muttered.

"After Guy's body washed up in Connecticut, there were an awful lot of people who thought he was killed as a hit by a rival group. It made them quickly make me the boss. You know, so there was no void in leadership. If it came out that he died trying to kill someone from his much talked about twenty-year-old rampage, the whole organization I took over would be a laughing stock. On top of that, they found Tony's body with a shitload of bullets in it."

"Yeah?"

"Well, it comes back that ballistics show that the bullets in Tony are from the same gun that killed Gyp and Rosalie DeAngelis six years ago. Now, you and I know who did that, but the fucking police can't make any sense of it."

"Poor cops," I said sarcastically.

"No, asshole. Nothing would make them conclude that Guy killed Tony. Therefore, they have to figure that Tony got shot while unsuccessfully protecting his brother from the same killer who murdered the DeAngelis couple."

"What's the problem?"

"They will have their suspect when they test the blood on the *Fun Ghoul* and find that it's. . ."

"Mine!"

"Bingo, asshole. Especially, since I made you the main suspect in the disappearance of their son, Gio, twenty-three years ago."

"Fuck you," I yelled defiantly.

"Funny way to talk to a guy who holds your life in his hands. You're lucky I need you to disappear rather than die. See, dead bodies have a tendency to pop up now and then. They can be tested."

"What?"

"If you are never seen again, and they can't match the blood to you, they got nothing. My bosses will still think that you are out there somewhere and give me free-reign to strengthen my power. However, if they find out Guy died trying to get mindless revenge for a stupid incident over two decades ago, as I said, my crew will be a laughing stock."

I looked at him and waited to hear my fate.

"So, here's the deal, Johnny "Fuckin'" Cipp, as my cousin called you. You leave town and never say a word to anyone about anything, and I'll let you go. In fact, I don't even want to know where you end up. I figure you got lost for twenty-three years the first time; you can do it again. The other choice is that I kill all of you."

"I'm OK with that," I answered, "I mean choice one, not the other one."

"I can get you out of here. I may be retired and outside my

jurisdiction, but *these* cops are all my people. I'll have you left off at Riet's house. The least she can do is help you after you saved her life. But remember, you never talked to me, you never met me, or else. And you can never step foot in New York again. Understand? Never!"

It wasn't like I had much choice, but I eagerly agreed. And so, I never would come up and see Riet or my old hometown again. Small price. A couple of his men somehow got me discharged then put me in a car before I knew what was going on. Once in the back seat, I found Richie Shea sitting next to me. This Richie seemed to be a kinder, gentler version of the person who had just put on a show in my hospital room. He said nothing for a few minutes and then stuck his hand in his coat pocket. *Oh shit, does he just want me out of the hospital to finish me off?* But then what he produced wasn't a gun.

"I want you to know that I had nothing to do with the deaths of your friends. I even felt bad helping cover up everything that happened. I felt like I knew each of them."

"Get off the fucking pot. You didn't know them. You knew nothing about them." I shouldn't have allowed myself to lose my temper with this guy who had just granted me my life, but I never acted rationally when it came to the guys. Still, Richie didn't lose his temper. In fact, his expression softened.

"Take this," and he handed me a picture of the band. "I've been carrying this around since Gyp DeAngelis gave this to me to help find his son and you. Every day I looked at it, knowing that four of those young faces were already dead and I was supposed to find the fifth and kill him. It did a number on my head."

"In the words of your former boss, fangul." I knew he was feeling something. I guess I am not the only one who can feel guilt, but I wasn't the forgiving type. "You want me to forget that you were leading Riet and Van to their deaths a few nights ago?" I was pissed off.

"No, I want you to remember in case you ever think of reneging on our deal—I'm going out on a limb here. I'm in deep shit if you ever show up again. I still can't figure out why the fuck I am doing it this way. I have never actually killed anyone and I don't want to start now. However, if it comes down to you or me, you're dead. Remember that."

I was fading in and out of consciousness and had difficulty sitting up in the car. I found out later I was left off at Riet's house. I could never explain to her how or why I was there. It was part of our deal. Just before they placed me in front of her house, Shea hesitated a second and then continued, "My going away present to you." He handed me the picture of the band, and I saw the faces that I hadn't seen in decades.

———◆———

For the next three days, I cherished that photo, the only one ever taken of the band. It had been snapped on the first warm spring day of 1967, two months before disaster struck and swept them all away. We were on a break after six hours of practice that Saturday afternoon and allowed ourselves to breathe in the warm air that had finally ended a very bitter winter. While we were standing around, Jimmy Mac's mother came out with an Instamatic camera in her hand and asked to capture the moment. Later she had given each of us a copy. I don't know what happened to my copy, but Gio's had stayed in his room until it had somehow found its way into Shea's hands and now mine. *Photographs and memories.*

It was Gio's idea to pretend it was the picture for the album cover we thought would soon be a reality. Though psychedelic covers had become the rage of the time, we decided to pose in a way that harkened back to those British Invasion groups that were so influential when we had started the whole thing.

We couldn't force a smile out of Bracko. Instead, we all tried to follow his lead and take on a sullen, troubled teen type of persona. Bracko stood to the left side of the group facing sideways. Only his guitar faced the camera. It was slung over his neck with his left arm pushing its neck towards the ground. His head was bowed, and his eyes looked at his guitar as if to say, *this is who I am.*

Though they tried to remain equally sullen, Jimmy Mac and Tinman struck a playful pose in the middle of the scene. Tinman Joey held no instrument but stood with his arms crossed in front of him. I always imagined that this reflected his wish to be seen as a person rather than just a keyboard player. Beside Joey and in the center of the group stood Jimmy Mac. His hands were held high with a drumstick in each. His attitude was the total opposite. He wanted the world to know that he was the drummer of Those Born Free, and damn proud of it. As much as they tried, neither one of them could wipe the slight smirks that began to form on their lips.

Gio and I stood on the right side of the picture. Both our instruments were placed with the edges of their bodies on the ground. They rose up with their necks coming up to our midsections where they leaned against our chests. I stood erect, my ankles crossed in a way that looked cool on the cover of a Kinks' album. Both my hands rested on the top of my bass guitar. Gio, in turn, had a similar pose but only had one hand on the top of his guitar, his other arm's elbow rested on my shoulder, and his hand curled back to his head in a look of casual fun. Against the attitude we had all agreed to, he also snuck in a slight smile. That was Gio.

When I think back now, I try forgetting all the evil that finished our story. I think back to the $20 Silvertone guitars and those first chords we ever played. I think of all the hopes and expectations. I see each of their faces as they were then. I can hear the sounds of us arguing over this chord or that note. I also hear the beautiful music that came from those arguments and compromises. I hear us laughing together. I'm sad once again that these sounds are all gone. They exist only in my memories. *Photographs and memories.*

———◆———

After those three days in 1990, I gave the photo to Van. I cherished the only remaining likeness of my band, but this was the only existing picture of his father. Now in 2013, he had made a copy of that picture and tucked it in my journal.

27

Journal of Johnny Cipp

Entry # 110 - February 15, 2013 - 5:37 p.m.

"Tonight, I Just Need My Guitar"
- *Jimmy Buffett*

S O HERE I AM AGAIN in the present. The Music Doctor mocks and tempts me to entitle this section "Dear Diary." For the second time in my life, I realize there isn't much more to write in this journal.

———◆———

I run my own little place down here now. I should've gone out of business long ago. In theory, I have no business being as successful as I am when you consider the premise of my venture. I own a bar that is *not* a bar. My little club offers excellent music because I pay top dollar to those who audition (with three forms of age ID, of course) and are good enough to make it to my stage.

Here is the catch though; I don't allow alcohol in my "bar." The proof requirement is just to keep it a mature establishment. We have some overpriced soda and some fruit smoothies. Anyone who comes into my place is here for the music and not the buzz. Many of my customers have heard about the club at the AA meetings at Mary of the Sea Church basement where I was recently honored for passing the quarter-century mark of sobriety. I make my money on a nice $10-a-head door charge. However, if you see me and tell me you love music, but don't have the money, I'll probably let you in for free.

I call my club *Those Born Free*. Under the marquee is a little explanation that the place is meant to be a haven for "Those born or reborn free of the need to be high to enjoy God's gift of music." Unbelievably, the concept is so different from every other club in the per capita drunk capital of the world, Key West, that I have cornered a niche market, making me financially independent. I like that. The idea I can spend my days around music, musicians, and lovers of music without starving is just about all I could wish for in life. Occasionally, I sit in with a little bass action and sometimes I might even do an acoustic set if there is a blank spot in a night's activities.

Even though it doesn't mean much to me anymore, I'm feeling safe these days. Only the people who read my journal know where I am hiding out and they won't tell. I see no reason to change my name again. The only price I pay for my security is never being able to return to home.

I still occasionally hang out at the baseball practices of Van's team. I would say I was there to offer my expertise, but I can't lie about that in my journal. Baseball has passed me by. I hang out there because Coach Van DeAngelis asks me to. Former coach, Cal Fremont, remains my closest friend in the world. Together we go to get some fresh air. We also scout Van's latest prospects. Sometimes I drive over to Cal's for dinner afterward. Very often I find there is a fourth to our dinner parties. Cal and his wife Hannah are continually trying to fix me up with someone who will end my damned loneliness.

I still spend some time with Padre. I occasionally supply him with a reclamation project addict he has somehow missed in his sweeps of Key West. I get a kick seeing some *fortunate* slob working at the menial tasks I once did around the church. Padre still dresses and wears his hair and beard like Jesus. Well actually, it's more like Jesus if he hadn't been crucified and had lived long enough to collect social security. The saintly father sometimes comes in to visit the club. What a group we make: the retired coach, the priest, and the ex-addict/musician. My new band of brothers.

Through the years, Van has come down to visit. Now he brings the whole family and sometimes I even go up to Homestead to spend a holiday with them. His kids call me "Uncle J" and I like that. I have a family. Whether it is one-on-one with Van down in my bar, or sitting around the kitchen table after a fantastic meal at his house, the conversation always takes a certain turn. I know what is coming when there is a bit of silence. Van will always look me in the eyes and say, "Tell me something about my father that you never told me before."

———◆———

Tonight, I will again perform at my club. I already know the opening act is going to be a little late showing up. This means that I will fill in for about a half an hour until they get there. I can predict what tonight will be like because I don't vary my repertoire much. The only part of my act that changes is how long I perform. My stage time is determined by the irresponsibility of the groups that I hire. I sometimes wonder if my ego makes me look for the bands that may not always show up on time.

I follow the same ritual every time I call upon myself to be on stage. First, I take two Aleve, the only pharmaceutical I allow myself these days. The fractures to my left hand have finally caught up with me in the form of the intense throbbing pain of arthritis. That was something that never occurred to me in the old days, and even today it seems so un-rock and roll.

I'm not limited to doing "Louie, Louie" six times. *And the audience screams for another encore of "Louie, Louie."* I sing a little better (with the emphasis on little) than I did back in the 60s in a raspy Kris Kristofferson sort of way. Usually, I only get through the chorus of that classic song once, and I end up leading a sing-a-long.

"Louie, Louie, oh babe, we gotta go . . ."

I have taught my regulars the lyrics to this song that had eluded so many of them for so long. There are usually comments like "so that's what they're singing in the song." I still laugh because I learned the words a half a century before by listening to the original unheralded 1955 version by Richard Berry. Now anyone with a computer can google the lyrics in a matter of seconds.

"The Doctor" by the Doobie Brothers follows "Louie, Louie." Though it loses something without the full, raucous sound of that group's instruments, it still means a great deal to me to sing that "music is the doctor and it makes me feel like I want to."

I follow these tunes with an original or two of which one of them is always requested to be "Gypsy Rose." Consider the audience! These are mostly recovering addicts of some form of chemical abuse. They usually chant the phrase, "Blew my mind," with an absurd amount of enthusiasm.

I follow this outburst by inserting the designated mind-altering experience that each verse contains. Though they are joyous and vibrant in their vocal contributions, there is a certain sadness evident in those audience members who recall how much they have hurt themselves and others in the past. It is a poignant moment when they bow their heads and raise their hands high to signify when I've hit upon their drug of choice. Too often hands are held high throughout the entire song.

Knowing my voice has only about three or four more songs left in it and my left hand even less, I will start to mellow the tone of the set at that point. The fourth song of my set will vary with my mood. The journal has returned, and I've spent much of the last few days reading it. This led me to believe I will not be playing anything joyful or uplifting. I will probably go with Clapton's "Tears in Heaven". Though he wrote it about his young son who was tragically lost in a fall from a window, the song is so ripe with meaning for my experience. *"Would you know my name, if I saw you in heaven?"*

Sometimes for that fourth song, I will do a very soft and touching version of Blue Oyster Cult's "Fear the Reaper." The newcomers in the crowd have never heard this song sung this slow and emotional. The song is about suicide. I try to remember how far I had fallen back in 1990.

Before I start the last song, I always perform a very personal ritual. Not understanding the meaning of my actions, the audience is always amused when I take my guitar from around my neck and look at the polished wood on the backside of the instrument. No one has ever seen what is there. Because of this peculiar habit, my regulars taunt me. I hear the catcalls that I'm so old that I've forgotten the lyrics. They lovingly berate me about my supposed need to use a cheat sheet. Only there are no lyrics to be found there. I know the last song by heart. I remember them as well as I know my name. Well, I guess that's a bad analogy.

The Aleve will have been defeated by my age and condition. Still, I must sing one more song. It is time to give the crowd a song that only I can perform here at Those Born Free Club. The irony isn't lost on me that it should've been done *by* Those Born Free instead of *at* Those Born Free Club. I will repeat the ritual of looking at the rear of the guitar and again hear the good-hearted jibes of my regulars. If they looked very carefully, they would notice that I'm now not just looking at the rear of the guitar but almost caressing it like a lover. Gio's guitar, the same one he never returned to claim, the same one he *could* never come back to claim. If he could have played it again, he would have smiled at what I had added to the back the instrument decades ago.

I will close out the voices of the audience from my consciousness. Instead, I will concentrate on my ritual, my one final act of commemoration. My eyes will once again fix on the one surviving Those Born Free business card. It has been taped to the rear of the guitar for so long that both the tape and card have started to yellow. As the friendly catcalls persist, I run my hands over the writing printed during more joyous times. Displayed around the perimeter of the card are the five names of a band that once was. "Jimmy Mac" McAvoy . . . "Bracko" Brackowski . . . and Joey "Tinman" Tinley. I pause to look at my name. Though I will never use it again, Johnny Cipp will always live inside of me.

As usual, I will pause for a split second before caressing the print above the letters G-I-O. I miss him most of all. I miss what was and what could have been.

Suddenly I turn around,
And all of it is lost.

Those five names were printed on the cards that we were so proud of but never got to share with the world. I guess my parents discarded the other 497 cards in a moment of great depression. One had been given to Bracko, and I don't know what happened to it. One had been given to Vinnie the Cat, and somehow never found its way to the lunatic who was his boss. And one sits here.

In 1990, I added one more name to the card. I used my best printing to inscribe one final addition to the only remaining artifact of the group. I tried to recreate the exact font that some long-forgotten professional printer had used to proclaim our names to the world. The letters T-O-N-Y sit in the midst of all the other departed names.

At that point, I will quickly give the guitar the same knocking sound that Tony so loved to hear Bracko tap on his guitar in the midst of playing "Knock on Wood." I will smile a bit before turning the ancient instrument over to play my final song. If the crowd looks close, they will see me tear up. The guys are all gone.

I put up with the good-natured heckling of the crowd, but I could never forget the words to "The Thief of My Forever." The words are ingrained in my soul as is every moment of that long ago afternoon when we came together to write it.

> *Sometimes I sit for hours,*
> *Thinking of times past.*
> *All those years of innocence,*
> *Have left me, gone so fast.*

I try to do justice to the opening guitar riffs that Bracko created for this song. The crowd usually likes how I play, but they've never heard the original. I sing and play with every ounce of effort my body can stand. The verses will flow and . . .

It is time for me to go on stage . . .

Entry #111– February 15 - 11:37 p.m.
(my final entry)

"Still Crazy After All These Years"
-Paul Simon

After I finished playing, I left my club. I decided to write in this journal sitting on this same lonely beach where Padre rescued first my soul . . . and then my body. I sit here often, just Gio's guitar and me. Tonight the journal has found its way back to me and so it sits by my side ready for my fare-well entry

The truest words ever written came four decades ago when we gave the "Thief" song its ending stanza.

In time, Time takes everything.

For the first time in a long while, I find myself not think-ing of the past but rather thinking of the future. All the lost years of my life have taken a toll on my body. I look realistically at the fact that my time on this planet has an expiration date. I have to face the reality I probably have less time left on this "cold, dark orb" (a final Moody Blues reference) than I ever lived under the name of Johnny Cipp. What then? What will happen to the memory of Those Born Free? Will it just drift away and be forgotten? Will the story finally be over?

I am not crazy. At least, I don't think so. Well . . . maybe a little. Still, I come here often to be with the band. I still see them in the clouds. As long as I do that, they remain alive to me. I will never know what happened to Jimmy Mac's tapes of the band, and I will never hear them really play. However, when I come here I can play the songs over and over again in my head and picture them in the sky above. However, the scene is slightly different than the one I envisioned all those years ago when I attempted to join them.

Yes, the band is still there in all its glory, playing with an enthusiasm I can almost feel. And yes, I wish I could join them, but I still have too much to accomplish in the world. But they are out there.

I look at Tinman as he wails on his organ. He lifts his head up from the keys and gazes out at the audience. Yes, there is an audience. Wild applause is seen and heard from his parents' Joseph and Margaret. They smile and wave to him.

Meanwhile, Stan Brackowski and Noel McAvoy are high-fiving and pointing to their sons. Gyp and Rosalie DeAngelis are more subdued; they are more recent ticket holders to this event. They are being comforted by another couple who have had decades to enjoy the music. It is my parents who soothe their angst with welcoming smiles and point up at my best friend. Gio's parents have finally found their son. His disappearance is no longer a mystery. I pause to look at the faces of my mom and dad with guilt. I never said goodbye.

Yet, the newer faces are not just in the audience. As the band plays on, I can't help but notice it has new players. Standing close behind Jimmy Mac stands Diane. As the drummer smiles at her, he taps lightly on his tom-tom drum. She laughs and answers with the syncopated beat of a tambourine. Jimmy Mac turns away because it's time to sing harmony again. But the harmony is not just with Gio. There is a now a new voice added to the mix.

Center stage Gio shares his mic with Riet. But I am not looking at the Riet who had been worn out by a hard life, or tortured by the rages of cancer. She is that beautiful young girl who stole Gio's heart and gave birth to his son . . . and to the band's name of Those Born Free. They are looking into each other's eyes and singing as if they are of one soul.

The guitar solo begins. Bracko, as usual, is playing with incredible skill. The notes ring with the sound of angels. It is not just the playing that entrances me. His smile engulfs the entire stage. His eyes have bright sparkles of happiness in them. When he sees he has my attention, his head shifts as if giving me an unspoken command to follow his line of sight over to his left. I follow his direction, and there sits Tony holding his old broken string-less ukulele, pretending to go into a solo instrumental break. He too is laughing with wild abandon.

Yes, they're all there enjoying themselves. The Music Doctor taps me on the shoulder. My imaginary band has been playing for a while now, and I have been listening. It occurs to me that I wasn't conscious of what they were singing. I can almost see the Music Doctor losing his patience with me. He wants me to understand he has been with me as long as I can remember. He was there when we chose the name Those Born Free, and he wants me to know that this band finally is free. Confused for a few moments, I can hear the words they are singing, but they mean nothing, and therefore I don't really *hear* them. Something about "Baton Rouge" and "dirty red bandana." Then it came to the chorus and suddenly the voices of Gio, Jimmy Mac, and Riet become crystal clear.

"Freedom's just another word for nothing left to lose . . ."

So, I guess, I'll never entirely be free. But's that's OK with me. They are, and that is good enough for me (and my Bobby Magee) — *I just figured out the song they were sing-*

ing. I'm at peace with everything that happened. I guess the only thing that bothers me is that when I am gone, we will all be forgotten. Yeah, Van will remember some of what I have told him about his father and all of us. And maybe somewhere out there Maria recalls a time that once was. But the reality is that all this will be gone when I am. All the feelings, all the success, all the failures . . . there will be no record of our story. No one will care.

The band now fades from the clouds, and there is silence on the beach. The tingling sensation again tells me that the Music Doctor wants to speak to me, He wants to educate me. He wants me to know that I am right. I am the last vestiges of something that was. . . but is not anymore. When I go, the memories of us will truly "fade to never."

He's laughing at the irony of the fact that it has taken me forty-six years to come upon the one line of a song. . . a song whose release by The Youngbloods came on the *very day* of our demise and spoke to the truth of our existence.

"We were but a moment's sunlight . . . fading in the grass."

ADDENDUMS

"Piece(s) of My Heart"
- Janis Joplin

Author's Note: "And So It Goes" – Billy Joel

The Story of the Music Doctor: "Music Is The Doctor" – Doobie Brothers

A Special Dedication: "Teach Your Children" – Crosby, Stills, and Nash

Song Lists: "Wrote a Song for Everyone" – John Fogerty

Preview: "Days of Future Passed" – The Moody Blues

AUTHOR'S NOTE

"And So It Goes"
- Billy Joel

Many of the Florida Keys' locations mentioned in this book were destroyed by Hurricane Irma on September 10, 2017. Just like the snowbirds that I poked fun at in this book, I often take long walks along the Overseas Highway around Sugarloaf Key. The winter of 2018 was a surreal vision of wrecked boats and trailers overwhelming the formerly picturesque water and mangrove lined road.

Mangrove Mama's survived, but the Sugarloaf campground across the street that had been my home for the last twelve winters, lay a barren wasteland with much of its contents now lying in the Gulf of Mexico and the Atlantic Ocean. Much of the bright blue waters of the Keys became even bluer as massive amounts of sand were deposited on top of fledgling mangroves and juvenile seagrass. On some beaches, "Johnny" would have had to almost venture out into shipping lanes if he wanted to attempt suicide in water deeper than his knees. Yet, like all things in nature this will pass and I still look forward to the panoramic views that led to many of the scenes of these first two books.

Band in the Wind and *Sound of Redemption* were at one time a single book that originally weighed in at 231,000 words. Once I realized that I myself did not like to read 900 page books, the decision was made to shorten and separate the story at what I considered a natural breaking point – Johnny's suicide attempt. After almost a decade of writing the original and then making adjustments, I was ready to leave behind the world of Johnny Cipp. There was no more to be written. I swore to myself that there was nothing left in me to tell about these characters.

Yet it came to me late one night that so many people's lives from the original books had been left hanging when Johnny made his exit from the Heights. I am often asked what ever happened to DJ . . . and Brother Christian, and the many others who found their way in and out of Johnny's life?

One night the idea came to me that the world had been an exciting place to live in from 1967 to present and Johnny had missed it by hiding out in Key West. However, all of the other characters who had been left behind had lived in that world. It was from this kernel of an idea that *Brotherhood of Forever* was born.

Besides, DJ Spinelli and Brother Christian, there were many whose lives were touched by the brief existence of Those Born Free. The names may not sound familiar without introduction, but Aylin McAvoy, Neil Connaughton, Marylou Casali, Freddy Resch, John Barlow, Greg Cincotta, Jack Leonardo, Davis Jones, Thad Carver and more had lived in the world that Johnny had missed. Assassinations, peace marches, Vietnam War, moon landing, Woodstock, 9/11 all colored the events that these "others" lived through.

DJ Spinelli will spend decades of his existence trying to unfold the mystery of his friend, Johnny Cipp. In this quest, he is joined by many others who traversed the world of Those Born Free and the Heights. Their lives intertwine against the backdrop of 20th Century events and their own individual circumstances.

THE STORY OF THE MUSIC DOCTOR

The Soundtrack of My Life
"(Music Is) The Doctor"
– The Doobie Brothers

Just as the first draft of Band in the Wind was being completed, a version of this article was published in "New York Newsday." This was not a coincidence. The Music Doctor who populates my books and my world received his name at that exact moment in 2013. However, he has existed for as long as I can remember. Like my fictional hero Johnny Cipp, I know that he has been there for all the important moments of my life.

———◆———

As long as I can remember, I have had this tendency to think that there was a song for every moment of my life. It became an inside joke between the world and me. I can find a title or a phrase to represent every event that I have lived through.

My pre-pubescent musical memories are vague. I know that in my home, the only music that was played were songs that were categorized as "Country and Western." That form of music is enormously different from the "Country" music of today. In those days, it was exactly as the title predicted— western tinged. It very often told stories of cowboys and other forms of rural life. How my father, a son of English immigrants and growing up in the whaling village of New Bedford, became enamored with this music always remained a mystery to me.

My mother, a definite fan of Frank Sinatra, just rolled her eyes as this music blasted from our little Victrola. One of my father's favorite songs was Eddie Arnold's "Cattle Call" which actually had lines about "cattle prowlin' and coyotes howlin'." Was the music doctor listening? I was too young. I simply don't know. However, I did develop a lifelong dedication to hamburger, steak, and all red meat!

My first confirmed sighting of the doctor occurred around the time I met my first girlfriend. We swore our undying love for each other to the tune of the Beatles' "Do You Want to Know a Secret." My memory is just not good enough to remember that far back. A bit later, the band that I was in had modest success and played in the Village and in Central Park and I found myself humming "So You Want to Be a Rock and Roll Star" by The Byrds. A close encounter with the draft board and the Vietnam War led me to listening to "I-Feel-Like-I'm-Fixin'-To-Die-Rag" by Country Joe and the Fish. "The Doctor" was reaching maturity.

Upon graduating college, I pursued my true life's desire to be a teacher. It was not an easy road as I put in my time as a substitute and a private school teacher before finally attaining a full time public school job. By then, the vinyl records of my youth had given way to the cassette tapes of the 1970s. As I drove to work the very first day of what would become a more than three-decade long career, I popped a cassette in the player and cranked it up to full volume for Jethro Tull's "Teacher."

By the time we were settled enough to marry, my wife and I had known each other nine years. The "Do You Want to Know a Secret?" girl had stuck with me through the good times and bad. Therefore, for our wedding song we fittingly chose "A Time for Us." It was three years later that we welcomed our first child and I listened frequently to a track on a recently released Moody Blues' album. The song entitled "The Eyes of a Child" proffered that "we are all part of the love that exists in the eyes of a child." By the time our third child was born the words became even more specific.

Mike and the Mechanics' "In the Living Years" lyrics were quite cryptic. To paraphrase, *I wasn't there that morning my father passed away. Later that year I thought I felt his spirit in my newborn baby's tears.* My father had died in July and my daughter was born that November.

Time passed, the kids grew, and life went on. When I coached all three of them in baseball and softball, and played softball myself, it seemed only fitting to play John Fogerty's "Centerfield" (a position we all played at one time or another). More than once I heard, "Put me in, Coach (Dad), I'm ready to play." The sports and music connection continued when I suffered a bout of midlife insanity and ran six marathons. All throughout the training and races, my headphones would blast the Grateful Dead's words that I had adopted . . . "I will survive." Ironically, the title of that song was actually "A Touch of Grey," which acknowledged the fact that heredity had left me with totally gray head by the age of forty.

There was no one who did not feel the tragedy of September 11, 2001. However, those of us who were born and raised in New York City perhaps felt a bit more emotion. Billy Joel's "New York State of Mind" and Bruce Springsteen's "My City of Ruin" seemed to reverberate in my ears during those dark days.

It was a brief four years later that I retired after 34 years of teaching. My cassette player had been replaced by a cd player, but I never forgot how I had pulled up to school that long ago first day playing "Teacher." I had really enjoyed my years as an elementary, middle school, high school, and college teacher, but it was time to relax and enjoy myself on a full time basis. After I said my final goodbyes and walked out of the school doors that last time, I got into my car. As I put the key in my Toyota, the music track that I had queued up in the morning filled the air with "School's Out For-ever" by Alice Cooper.

My wife and I retired on that same day and looked for-ward to the free time together. I could not help but think of the John Lennon/ Mary Chapin Carpenter song "Grow Old Along with Me" (the best is yet to be). Yet our retire-ment had a much more specific theme song. Our dream had always been to buy an RV and achieve two very specific goals – to visit all 48 contiguous states and see every major league baseball park. In the ensuing years, we have taken 37 lengthy trips in our motorhome to achieve these goals. Reli-giously, each trip begins with the playing of Willie Nelson's "On the Road Again." In 2011, we entered our 48th state to the of sound "California Dreamin'" streaming through the speakers of our Winnebago. Our second goal came to fruition the next year.

Yet our golden years were also about our family and those three kids who had spurred so many of their own themes. They were now all adults. What was more fitting than to dance with my daughter at her wedding to Andrea Boccel-li's "Time to Say Goodbye?" And when each of my sons became fathers within a few months of each other, I was now faced with a third generation on which to inflict my musical musings. By 2009, technology (and free time) allowed me to create music videos to present to them on the occasion of their first Father's Day. One, I gave the Darius Rucker song "It Won't Be Like This For Long," while the other I gave Brad Paisley's "Anything Like Me" (*It's safe say that, they'll be payback if he's anything like me*).

In 2012, the soundtrack for the movie *Act of Valor* was released. Each song had to do with the deployment, actions, and return from action of troops deployed to the War on Terror. In August of 2012 my son Jarrod, an Army officer, left for Afghanistan. There are at least five or six songs on the album that expressed feelings that everyone in the family was going through during this time. I focused on the Winona Judd song "Whatever Brings You Back." On Memorial Day 2013, he returned safely to American soil and we all breathed a sigh of relief.

A year later, my wife Marilyn and I celebrated our birthdays two days apart. That week we shared another Beatles' song in the soundtrack of our lives. What could be more appropriate than *Will you still need me, will you still feed me* "When I'm 64?"

The vinyl records, cassette tapes, and cd's are all now consigned to long forgotten storage areas of my house. Everything is digital now. Everything has changed. Well, almost everything. That girl who shared the Beatles' song with me 54 years ago is still there after 47 years of marriage. The music doctor is playing one final song that summarizes all the music and living that have come before. In 2010, George Strait released a song based roughly on a Maya Angelou poem. Upon hearing it the first time, I realized that The Music Doctor was trying to tie it all together.

"Life's not the breaths you take, it's the moments that take your breath away."

A SPECIAL DEDICATION

"Teach Your Children"
– Crosby, Stills, and Nash

This book is dedicated to my parents William John Rostron, Sr. (Bill) and Josephine Paradiso Rostron (Peppy).

When my mom passed away last year at almost 95 years of age, my sisters and I had the task of emptying a life's worth of belongings from her apartment. It was there that I came upon the yellowed copies of every article that I had published in the last forty years. She had placed them in a box after showing them to her friends. I am glad that I made her proud because she was the one who always insisted that I get the college education that she felt the Depression deprived her of achieving. However, she never totally gave up the dream she had as child of becoming a teacher. Until the age of 86 she worked in the library of Suffolk County Community College. She helped students do their research in pursuit of the degrees that I know she valued so highly. When our entire family tried to dissuade her from working at all, her answer was simple.

"I don't need to do this. I do this because I enjoy being there with the kids and helping." She had hit upon the definition of a teacher.

My father never earned a degree either and did not even graduate high school. Instead, he chose to join the navy at age 17, eventually rising to the level of Chief Petty Officer. Yet, despite his lack of a formal education, he was an incessant reader. When I was young and enamored with the newly popular phenomena known as TV, he would always insist that it should not replace the habit of reading. Being a smug, know-it-all preteen, I argued this fact.

One day he sat me down with the TV in front of us and a book in his hand. We always watched "Gunsmoke" together and he asked me what I saw on the screen at that very moment. I shrugged and he pushed me harder to answer.

"What exactly did you see?"

"Well, the bad guy pulled out his gun and tried to shoot Marshal Dillon. But he was too slow and the marshal shot him first."

Much to my distress, he turned off the TV. In those days there were no such things as VCRs or DVRs or streaming, and so this meant that we would miss the episode. However, I guess that there was also a bit of a teacher in my father. He then pulled out the western novel that he was reading at the time and started to read.

Jack Barton reached down toward his newly shined leather holster. His youthful hand tried to retrieve his 1847 Colt Walker Revolver. His palm had barely begun to caress the wooden stock of the gun when he realized that he was too late. His gun would never kill another human being. The nine notches carved into the wooden grip would forever be his final total.

The sheriff placed his gun back at his side, its task completed. He did not rejoice at the death of his foe. His lightning fast reflexes had merely completed the job he was paid to do. There was no joy in killing for him. It was just something necessary.

I realized at the moment that I would be a lifelong reader. Eventually, I began a career that involved teaching reading and writing. I only hope that I instilled in my students some small semblance of a love of reading that I felt that day and that carried through the rest of my life.

SONG LIST 1

"Wrote a Song for Everyone"
- John Fogerty

BAND IN THE WIND

Asterisk (★) denotes the title has specific lyrics within the song that tie into the story line.

The version of the song noted is not always the original. It is the version preferred by the author.

Prologue and Part 1
1. Dancing on the Other Side of the Wind – Chris Delaney and the Brotherhood Blues Band
2. Night Moves – Bob Seger and the Silver Bullet Band
3. When I Was Young – The Animals ★
4. Where Have All the Good Times Gone – The Kinks★
5. The Doctor – Doobie Brothers★
6. Eyes of a Child – Moody Blues ★
7. Keepin' the Faith – Billy Joel ★
8. I Saw It on TV – John Fogerty ★
9. Love Potion #9 – The Searchers
10. You Really Got Me – The Kinks ★
11. Coming Generation – The Knickerbockers ★
12. We Gotta Get Out of This Place – The Animals ★
13. Changes – Moby Grape

14. Wonderful Tonight – Eric Clapton ★
15. Bus Stop – The Hollies ★
16. The Eve of Destruction – Barry McGuire
17. The Other Side of Life – Moody Blues ★
18. Out in Streets – Shangri-Las ★
19. Remember the Days in the Old Schoolyard – Cat Stevens ★
20. Bad to the Bone – George Thorogood and the Delaware Destroyers ★
21. Strange Days – The Doors ★
22. End of the Innocence – Don Henley
23. Sympathy for the Devil – Rolling Stones
24. Last Chance – John Mellencamp
25. I Want to Hold Your Hand – The Beatles
26. Tear Drops Will Fall – John Mellencamp
27. Centerfield – John Fogerty ★
28. Dancing in the Dark – Bruce Springsteen
29. Playing with Fire – Rolling Stones
30. While My Guitar Gently Weeps – George Harrison ★
31. My Hometown – Bruce Springsteen ★
32. I Can't Keep from Cryin' Sometimes – Ten Years After
33. True Love Ways – Buddy Holly ★
34. Street Fightin' Man – Rolling Stones
35. Accidently Like a Martyr – Warren Zevon
36. All Along the Watchtower – Jimi Hendrix
37. Takin' Care of Business – Bachman-Turner Overdrive
38. A Different Drum – Stone Ponies
39. The Loner – Neil Young★
40. Roll Over Beethoven – Chuck Berry
41. Crossroads – Eric Clapton
42. Lost in a Lost World – Moody Blues
43. Saved by the Music – Justin Hayward and John Lodge
44. House of Rising Sun – The Animals
45. Teacher – Jethro Tull

46. Something Better Beginning – The Kinks
47. No Time Like the Right Time – Blues Project
48. In the City – Joe Walsh ★
49. Knock on Wood – Eddie Floyd ★
50. You Can't Always Get What You Want – Rolling Stones
51. Summer in the City – Lovin' Spoonful ★
Part 2
52. Come Together – The Beatles ★
53. How Much I Lied – Gram Parsons
54. Bungle in the Jungle – Jethro Tull
55. I'm a Man – Bo Diddley/Yardbirds
56. Mr. Downchild – Savoy Brown ★
57. I May Be Wrong, But I won't Be Wrong Always – Ten Years After
58. In the Midnight Hour – Rascals
59. Liar, Liar – The Castaways
60. Train Kept a'Rollin' – The Yardbirds ★
61. All Day and All of the Night – The Kinks
62. Whiter Shade of Pale – Procul Harum
63. Heart Full of Soul – The Yardbirds
64. Something in the Air – Thunderclap Newman
65. Louie, Louie – The Kingsmen ★
66. Satisfaction – Rolling Stones
67. Money – The Beatles ★
68. Hero – David Crosby★
69. Summertime Blues – Blue Cheer ★
70. Keep On Dancin'— The Gentrys
71. Gypsy Rose – Those Born Free ★
72. Born Under a Bad Sign – Cream ★
73. We Ain't Got Nothin' Yet – Blues Magoos
74. Under the Boardwalk – The Drifters
75. Money – Pink Floyd
76. Miracles – Jefferson Starship

77. Summer Song – Chad and Jeremy
78. Hard Day's Night – The Beatles
79. Society's Child – Janis Ian ★
80. Name Game – Shirley Ellis
81. Just Like Romeo and Juliet – The Reflections
82. Pretty Flamingo – Manfred Mann
83. Heroes in the Night – Chris Delaney
84. So You Want to Be a Rock n' Roll Star – The Byrds ★
85. Blinded by the Light – Manfred Mann
86. Gloria – Shadows of the Knight
87. Gimme Some Lovin' – Spencer Davis Group
88. Year of the Cat – Al Stewart
89. Love Minus Zero – Bob Dylan
90. Break On Through – The Doors
91. On the Road Again – Canned Heat
92. Forever Autumn – Justin Hayward
93. On the Threshold of a Dream – Moody Blues
94. See My Friends – The Kinks
95. Thief of My Forever – Those Born Free
96. Who Are You? – The Who
97. Hey Gyp – The Animals
98. Do You Wanna Dance? – Mamas and Papas
99. Love Hurts – Everly Brothers
100. Words of Doubt – DJ Spinelli ★
101. The Piano – Joey "Tinman" Tinley ★
102. Enchanted Days – Those Born Free ★
103. Slow Dancin' – Johnny Rivers ★
104. Wishin' and Hopin' – Dusty Springfield
105. The Night Before – The Beatles
106. Talk, Talk – Music Machine★
107. Time Has Come Today – Chambers Brothers
108. Catch the Wind – Blues Project ★★★
   Part 3
109. When the Music's Over – The Doors ★

SONG LIST 2

SOUND OF REDEMPTION

Prologue and Part 11

1. I May Wrong, But I Won't Be Wrong Always –
    Ten Years After
2. Wake Me, Shake Me – Blues Project ★
3. Stairway to Heaven – Led Zeppelin
4. And the Tide Rushes In – Moody Blues ★
5. Knockin' On Heaven's Door – Bob Dylan ★
6. You May Be Right, I May Be Crazy – Billy Joel ★
7. The Walk of Life – Dire Straits ★
8. Honesty – Billy Joel ★

Part 2

9. Time Passages – Al Stewart ★
10. Lost Little Girl – The Doors ★
11. Listen to the Music – Doobie Brothers ★
12. I-Feel-Like-I'm-Fixin'-To-Die – Country Joe and the
    Fish ★
13. Bad to the Bone – George Thorogood and the
    Delaware Destroyers★
14. Madman Across the Water – Elton John
15. Birthday – The Beatles
16. Sad Little Girl – Beau Brummels ★
17. See My Friends – The Kinks ★
18. The Loner – Neil Young ★

Part 3

19. Turn the Page – Bob Seger and the Silver Bullet Band
20. Synchronicity – The Police

21. Take Me Out to the Ballgame – Jack Norworth
22. Johnny Angel – Shelley Fabares
23. You've Got a Friend – James Taylor
24. All Right Now – Free ★
25. The End – The Doors
26. Against All Odds – Phil Collins
27. Question of Balance – Moody Blues
28. Redemption Song – Bob Marley
29. Turn, Turn, Turn – The Byrds ★
     Part 4
30. Lives in the Balance – Jackson Browne ★
31. I Going Home – Ten Years After
32. Homeward Bound – Simon and Garfunkel
33. My Little Town – Simon and Garfunkel
34. In My Life – The Beatles
35. Money for Nothing – Dire Straits
36. Showdown – Doobie Brothers ★
37. Time Is Here and Gone – Doobie Brothers ★
38. Long Time Gone – Crosby, Stills, and Nash
39. Sounds of Silence - Simon and Garfunkel
40. With a Little Help from My Friends – The Beatles ★
41. Here in the Conch Republic – Howard Livingston
42. Photographs and Memories – Jim Croce
43. Tonight I Just Need My Guitar – Jimmy Buffet ★
44. Still Crazy After All These Years – Paul Simon
45. Me and Bobby McGee – Janis Joplin
46. Get Together – The Youngbloods ★

     Addendums
47. And So It Goes – Billy Joel ★
48. The Doctor – Doobie Brothers★
49. Teach Your Children – Crosby, Stills, and Nash★
50. Wrote a Song for Everyone – John Fogerty
51. Days of Future Passed – The Moody Blues

PREVIEW

"Days of Future Passed"
- The Moody Blues

———◆———

Coming Soon . . .

BROTHERHOOD OF FOREVER
Band in the Wind
Book 3

ACKNOWLEDGMENTS

Special thanks to **The Killion Group**

Kim Killion: cover design

Jenn Jakes: Formatting and so much more

E. M. Effingham, "The Word Chopper": Editing

And thanks to my proofreaders:
Mike Burdick, Robert Cappuccio,
and Marilyn T. Rostron.

———◆———

Contact William John Rostron:
BandintheWind@gmail.com

Join the Facebook Group:
BAND IN THE WIND

**Video of staged performance of "Pretty Flamingo"
from *Band in the Wind* on YouTube- "Visible Ink Pretty
Flamingo"**

SNEAK PEEK OF
BROTHERHOOD OF FOREVER

———

PROLOGUE

"Tonight's the Night"
- Neil Young

February 2015

HE LOOKED INTO THE MIRROR and evaluated his appearance. He had been going for the "cool with a touch of class" look. Though not usually vain, he realized that tonight millions of people would hear him. Talk about pressure. He had to do this right. It was important to him. It was important to them—all of them—the living and the dead.

One last look at his notes was in order. He had to make sure that he gave credit to everyone who deserved it before he went into the core of his speech. He would tell the story that had never been told before. He had to do it right.

"You almost ready?" His wife was in the next room and though he heard her, he did not immediately answer. He looked down at the iPod that sat in the Bose speaker in his bedroom. The fossilized cassette tapes that he had once held so dear were now all converted to digital entries on the iTunes app of his computer. As a tribute to the past he still labeled each one of the "songs" on the playlist as "cassette message" with the date that had been written on the original. Sometimes that information had not been available and the fading tapes only listed a month and year, or maybe the title of a song. He was so mesmerized by the list that he hardly heard the soft feminine voice that was now right next to him.

"One last listen before the big night?"

"Yeah," was his only reply.

"I think this one is the most fitting," she said as she reached over and pressed the iPod icon title that said very simply, "June 3, 1967."

"Yeah, that one says it all."

"If . . . if only he were still alive, he would get it."

"But he's not, and we have to learn to live with that."

She cried and hugged her husband tightly.

THOSE BORN FREE Tape - June 3, 1967

"Let's start at the beginning." (Johnny Cipp)

"Where else would we start, asshole?" (laugh)" (Gio DeAngelis)

"This song is a story, of course, we will start at the beginning. Well, actually, all songs are stories" (Joey "Tinman" Tinley)

"Are you done with the philosophy lesson, Tinman?" (Gio)

"I'm just saying that it is good to start a story at the beginning." (Tinman)

"Are you ready Bracko? Jimmy Mac?" (Johnny)

"Yup." (Bracko)

"Hold on a sec . . . I need to make sure the tape recorder is on. . . Oops! It's already on." (Jimmy Mac)

"You and those damn tapes." (Johnny)

"You're just jealous because you aren't singing on them. Or maybe we should just do "Louie, Louie" a few times? (laugh—Gio)

"We all have our strengths and weaknesses. You want to go a few innings of stickball, Gio?" (Johnny)

"Tooch, Touch, tootsie, . . . whatever the hell that word is for "you got me back." (Gio)

"You mean touché? Obviously, vocabulary is another challenge for you. (Johnny)

"Ha, ha, ha. . . and fuck you." (Gio)

"Ha, ha, ha, and fuck you and the horse you rode in on too!" (Johnny)

"Hey, my sisters are here!" (Jimmy Mac)

"Oops" (Johnny and Gio)

"Maggie and Siobhan are upstairs . . . and you think I don't know that word? Well, then fuck you, brother dear, I'm sixteen, you know." (Aylin McAvoy)

"Aylin!" (Jimmy Mac)

"Little sis is all grown up, Jimmy Mac" (Johnny)

"Yeah, fuck you, brother dear! What are you going to do? Tell Mom when she gets home from the store?" (Aylin)

"Aylin!" (Jimmy Mac)

"Someday. . . some guy is going to have his hands full with that girl." (Johnny)

"Jimmy Mac! Are you ready yet?" (Gio)

"Since your uncle gave you all those blank tapes it seems like you are taping every moment that we practice . . . why?

"I want us, the five of us, Those Born Free, to be remembered . . . forever." (Jimmy Mac)

"Forever?" (Johnny)

"Yeah. . . forever." (Jimmy Mac)

"Then forever, it is." (Gio)

"Forever." (Tinman)

"Forever." (Johnny)

"Bracko, ready to start us off?" (Johnny)
"Yup. . .oh yeah—forever!" (Bracko)
"Well said, Bracko, well said." (Gio)

Printed in the USA
CPSIA information can be obtained
at www.ICGtesting.com
LVHW021205300924
792512LV00006B/186/J

9 781732 746862